SAUSALITO

Sausalito.
Copyright © 2020 by Patrick J. Hagan

This is a work of fiction. Names, characters, places and incidents are either products of the author's imagination or are used fictitiously. Any resemblance to actual events, locales or persons, living or dead, is entirely coincidental.

Cover Image from the Original Painting
"Sausalito" by Howard Behrens
Courtesy Judi Behrens
For information visit www.HowardBehrens.com

ISBN 13
978-1-63132-109-2

Library of Congress Control Number: 2020919931

Library of Congress Cataloging-in-Publication Data
is available upon request.

First Edition

Published in the United States of America by ALIVE Book Publishing
an imprint of Advanced Publishing LLC
3200 A Danville Blvd., Suite 204, Alamo, California 94507
alivebookpublishing.com

PRINTED IN THE UNITED STATES OF AMERICA

10 9 8 7 6 5 4 3 2 1

SAUSALITO

PATRICK J. HAGAN

ABOOKS
Alive Book Publishing

DEDICATION

This, my first novel, is dedicated to those who have supported me over the years. At times they have given me love and encouragement, proven long-suffering, but always willing to help. They include my wife, Margaret Mary Lynch Hagan, my daughters, Jennifer Hagan and Kristin Hagan Sprincin, and my grandchildren, Katherine Hagan Sprincin, Patrick Hagan Sprincin, and Michael Sprincin.

This story is also dedicated to the men and women who have, over the years served in the United States Coast Guard, and especially to those associated with its Officer Candidate School Class of 1967 from USCG RESTRACEN Yorktown; and to all of those who serve and protect our American values and Constitution in the Armed Services of these United States of America, and especially to three: H. Kendall Felix, deceased, of Wilmington, Delaware (and roommate during their Plebe Year of John McCain), J. Charles Bradford, deceased, of Auburn, California, and MAJ Phillip Sprincin, USMC, of San Francisco, my son-in-law, all three of whom graduated during various times in its history from the U.S. Naval Academy.

ACKNOWLEDGMENTS

Bruce McDonald was an OCS classmate of mine in January of 1967 and we served three years together at USCG Headquarters, then 1300 Pennsylvania Avenue (my vantage point to see the Inauguration Parade Of Harry S. Truman in 1949), where we became life-long friends for his encouragement and insights in this writing project, especially in the detailed editing of *Sausalito* where he was invaluable; and to the Honorable Kristin Carson Hoffman, a Hastings Law School study group partner, and her husband, Bob, for reading drafts and supplying comments: and to my former law partner, E. Jane Wells, for her comments and encouragement.

To all of those partners at Dillingham & Murphy LLP, where I came on board with a team in 1995, and from which I retired at the end of 2019, and especially to Peter Torp, Ranita Prasad, and Debbie Ardissone Peterson, and in Memory of William Otis Dillingham, UCSF Hastings School of Law 1976, a dear friend.

Lastly my thanks to Phillip Sprincin, always ready to help, especially in overcoming my technical competence shortcomings, to his parents, and to my wife and daughters.

PROLOGUE

*D*ear Ronan, By the time you receive this package, I will have been gone at least 3 months. You will doubtless be surprised to hear from me, so an explanation is in order.

When we first met, I thought of you as just another patient ... and that lasted for a number of years, although our sessions revealed a man with a most troubled past. However, the years nurtured our relationship, at least from my perspective. Certainly, you became aware that we were more than doctor/patient at some point. Though I cannot say precisely when it occurred, we also became friends.

What I do not think you ever realized is that over all these years and our many sessions, I came to really care about you. Yet I never had the sense that you saw me as any more than a doctor who treated you and over the years became your friend. I got to the point, at times, when our sessions would go on hiatus because of your work, or your travels, or whatever, that I would play back sessions from different times. The earliest ones, from the point of later years, moved me to a different understanding of who you were, and how you became what you are.

Ronan-You have had a complex life. You have had a myriad of experiences - many of them troubling — which you shared with me, and probably no one else. Certainly not all of them. As you know, I taped many of our sessions, but there were some that you requested I not do so. For those, I took notes. The accompanying package is all of your tapes, all of my notes, and all of my analyses and musings. I send this all to you after considered thought. Your story is yours. Your experiences and knowledge are unique. In all, you are a good person, but flawed, as are all of us. The difference is your story is worth telling. As your doctor, I could never do that. Only you can. You have all of the *source material you will need. Tell what you will, in whatever order you think appropriate. I offer only one suggestion in that regard: start when you first came to Sausalito.*

That's enough. I am tired now and know I will be gone soon. I have instructed my lawyer to send this to you after I am gone 3 months. Know that I died thinking of you,

With my love,

Margo Arnaut, M.D.

It all began with the girl on the bike-

DR. ARNAUD'S REQUEST

When I first crossed that span across the body of water called the Golden Gate, the late afternoon winter fog was beginning to gather close to the water's surface. Following the directions given me by phone, I was able to leave the main highway after crossing the bridge, followed a series of turns through an inactive Army installation, turned park land, and came to a spot on the unpaved roadway where a number of vehicles were parked. A few hundred feet below I could see activity and a black surge pulsing against the shoreline. I was in the right area. Leaving my Dodge Charger, I clambered down the makeshift path toward the base of the steep hill where a bit of a beach contained many people gathering seabirds, cleaning them, or in some cases putting them in cages, apparently for transportation elsewhere. A few men in Coast Guard work uniforms appeared to be gathering samples of the offending toxins which was reported to be unrefined oil. After taking some photographs and speaking with the men in uniform, I knew that this was one of many sites along the northern edge of San Francisco Bay that had been contaminated by the collision between two oil tankers about 13 hours ago. The light was fading, but I had gotten to the scene on the same day as the accident. My goal was partly achieved. Other goals awaited the next days.

Joel Tinker had written some months ago that he had found an apartment in Sausalito not far from the Golden Gate Bridge. When I called to tell about my sudden trip, he asked me to stay with him and quickly explained how to get to his place from my approximate location. In the slowly gathering darkness, I made my way up the slope without dirtying my uniform, pulled out my notes with Tinker's directions and started to retrace my steps back to the main roadway which had turned off U.S. 101 to Sausalito, but then I made a left turn to begin toward the town. After going no more than a few hundred yards, and while getting my bearings in this new area, a woman bicyclist passed me on the left. She was really moving, had no helmet and I could see her blonde hair streaming behind her. Going slightly slower and watching for my turn-off, I lost sight of her after a few turns on the curvy downhill road. Suddenly, civilization appeared. Houses went up the hill on the left and driveways appeared on the right. The sign for Cote d'Azur appeared suddenly as Tinker had said it would. I braked hard and made a quick right turn onto a rooftop parking deck. Just a few feet away, that same blonde woman was locking up her bike. I asked her where I might park. She was pleasant, nice. Asking me whom I was going to see, she gave me instructions on where to park and said she would wait for me to show me how to get to Tinker's apartment as the complex was unusually laid out.

The blonde woman watched me exit my car, put on my uniform jacket and cap, then stand erect to my full 6'5" She put out her hand and said. "Hi, I'm Carolyn Tyne." After my introduction and a few questions and pleasantries, we were at Tinker's door. I wasn't sure what to say, so I thanked her. As she started to leave, she turned and said that she would be at the No Name Bar on Bridgeway about 9:00 that night. With that she was gone. She was tall and I'm 6'5"!

Tinker opened his door within seconds of my knock. He was dressed in civvies. Of course, he was. He had left active duty. We had met during Coast Guard officer training and been reunited little more than a year ago at Coast Guard HQ in Washington, D.C. Now, he was a first year law student at a little known University of California school called Hastings College of Law. He still looked fit, but he had more hair and what looked like the beginnings of a beard and mustache! Our mutual greeting was lengthy. Much had happened in the 6 months since last

I saw Tinker. He had left the Guard and I had taken over his job at USCG HQ in the Special Ops branch of the Office of Operations while he was moving to California to begin a new life. We had drinks, talked and began catching up. He told me about law school, his various classes, the amount of work, his interactions with the faculty and with his fellow students. He spent more time than needed on one student and at last suggested that I might meet her at dinner the next night. I asked him about the blonde woman. He knew about whom I was asking without hesitation. Tinker said she was a model and was here when he arrived. She went on assignments, had a bevy of friends, and was pleasant every time he met her.

Before I could mention the No Name, he suggested a quick dinner which he had prepared and explained that he would need 3 or 4 hours to prepare for tomorrow's classes. With that, I decided that I would make a foray to the No Name Bar.

***

Sitting at the bar of the easily located establishment on Bridgeway, Sausalito's main bayside street, I began to realize that I had a bit more to drink than was my usual, or even special, evening fare. So, I nursed my sidecar while I waited to see if Carolyn Tyne would actually show up. By 9:20, I began to seriously consider that the balance of my night would be spent alone.

Moments later, in walked a group of 5 or 6, among them, Carolyn. They gravitated toward the back of the large room where the bar ended and only tables were available. As they began to take seats, Carolyn looked in my direction, said something to the group, and began to move in my direction. As she got close, I stood up, not quite certain what to do next. She came right up to me, gave me a bit of a hug, a peck on the cheek, and said, "Ronan, I'm so glad you could make it here. I told my friends I might not be right back."

With that I offered her my stool, but the man to my right quickly slid over one stool, and seeing his gesture, Carolyn and I both sat. She asked what I was trying, and hearing a Sidecar, she quickly ordered two "Between the Sheets," explaining that a shot of rum gave the drink better taste and a lot more zest. We talked companionably for a few minutes. She told me how she had loved my uniform and was surprised to learn that I was in the Coast Guard and not the Navy. Then she said I had looked so handsome. I was embarrassed. The drinks arrived. We talked about the assignment that had brought me to Sausalito and about Tinker. Our drinks seemed to vanish and with that I told her I had better leave by 10:00 as I had to be in San Francisco at 7:30 next morning. She asked if I drove down the hill to the bar. When I said I had walked, she nodded and said she would drive me back to the apartments. She went over to her friends for a quick consult and was back in no time.

She had a Mustang convertible with the top up. She hopped in the driver's side, put the top down,.and in moments we were back on the rooftop lot. She glanced at her watch and said, "It's only 9:50. Can you come down for a quick nightcap?" I thought for just a second and said, "Yes," with some enthusiasm. The rest of that night remains a blur. I know I really did have too much to drink, that Tinker was not happy when I finally got in, and that Carolyn had had her way with me.

Tinker forgave me when we got together early the next evening. He also handed me a handwritten note that he said he found in his mailbox when he got back from school. Carolyn wrote:

"Ronan- Am off to a shoot in the Caribbean. Doubt I will run into you there. Great night! Hope to see you again. Carolyn —- P.S. My address and phone number are on my card in the envelope."

1

THE ASSIGNMENT

I spent 3 more days in the San Francisco area. Both of the tankers were damaged, but readily available for inspection. Officers from the Twelfth Coast Guard District Office Maritime Safety Branch (e.g.,CCGD12(m)) and Engineering as well as Legal arranged to make a detailed survey of the 2 damaged vessels on successive days. Other federal government agencies were represented as well as various California and regional investigative agencies. As a representative of the Commandant's Office of Operations (COMDT(O)), I was to be part of the overall team. This was my second disaster as I had been sent to observe a tanker run aground in San Juan Harbor, Puerto Rico, within days of my arrival back at USCG HQ. My job was to take photographs, listen to those in the know, assess what were the paramount issues and come up with a big picture perspective for the top operational brass at HQ, especially in Operations and the Chief of Staff.

After spending a few morning hours observing and photographing more sullied beaches, seabirds and other creatures, we proceeded to Richmond, CA. where the Texaco tanker was berthed. Its bow was a mess as it had run into the Chevron tanker amidships. A tour took more than an hour with a careful review of the damage to the ship's structure, including that the force of the collision appeared to rupture a forward tank. Other than the yard hand who provided access to the tanker, no one from Texaco was present.

The next day was a different ship yard and a different ship with far more damage where it had been struck amidships but the hull did stay intact sufficiently to allow it to be towed to safety; however, the crude oil in all but one of its tanks had emptied into San Francisco Bay in what the newspapers were calling a disaster of epic magnitude. Again, no one from Chevron was present to assist in the inspection. Both of these were preliminary inspections and teams would go over the tankers in far more detail in the days and weeks to come.

As a group, we then journeyed to the San Francisco Bay Traffic Control Center atop Yerba Buena Island. Here, our task was to interview the Coast Guard watch standers on duty at the time of the event: a Lieutenant (LT), a first class quartermaster (QM1), and a second class radar man (RN2). The facility was equipped with surface search radar to track ship movements as well as radios with which to communicate with shipping traffic. Major ship movements, including these 2 tankers would file departure schedules days ahead of time with the USCG Captain of the Port (COTP) for San Francisco. Charts of the Bay with clearly defined lanes for inbound and outbound traffic had existed for many decades, while internationally agreed upon Rules of the Road had existed for more than a hundred years governing ingress and egress to all U.S. ports. Both tankers also had San Francisco Bay pilots on board.

These interviews of the Coast Guard's own were to be the first of many over the ensuing weeks. Their story was straight forward: all ship movements were as expected until about 90 seconds before the collision. There was low fog at, and under, the Bridge. However, with both ships equipped with their own radar, they should not have had a problem. Instead, there were a series of last second unapproved course corrections, each seemingly in anticipatory response to the other ship's course changes which combined to bring the two tankers together. The course correction commands happened so quickly and the actual course heading changes from the tankers were so slow that Traffic Control was essentially helpless to prevent the tragedy.

My last day was to observe the initial interviews of each captain of the two colliding vessels I thought I knew what to expect but what happened changed the course of my life!

2

JOHN BARLEYCORN

Tinker arranged an evening in the City for my second night in the Bay Area, specifically for me to meet his girlfriend. He was already near the meeting place, a restaurant of sorts called John Barleycorn, apparently a short distance from University of California, Hastings College of Law (UC Hastings) where they both went to law school. Following his careful directions, I made it to the area and eventually found a parking space near California Street. Cable cars ran right past the restaurant as I walked the few final blocks. Upon entering, I spotted Tinker at a table. He was facing the door. With him, their backs to me were two women - one a blonde, the other a brunette. As I approached Tinker rose. When he did, so did the two women. Both turned to face me as I covered the final two steps.

Tinker gestured and introduced the brunette first. She was Elaine Smart, tall, pleasant of face and spare of frame. By the look they exchanged, I could tell that theirs was more than just friendship. Elaine and I shook hands warmly, being January, I was cold from the short walk. Elaine greeted me effusively and turning to the blonde woman said, "This is my friend Sandra Allen. I hope you don't mind that I brought her along, but she has heard so much about you and her being here means I won't have to repeat the night's events to her."

That said, all three of them began to speak at once, but deferred to Elaine after a moment. She began to cover my background about Tinker and I having served together for a year at USCG HQ and then, looking at me, said, "Tinker never uses the word, but it would seem you are a war hero. We don't get many military types at Hastings. Tinker is one of the few and he never saw combat."

It was like Elaine wanted me to say something to that, but I wasn't sure what. Before Tinker could verbally step in, Sandra sitting across from me, quickly interjected, "I'm sure you have a great deal to remember about your time in Viet Nam. Tinker told us about your medal, but you don't have to talk about how you got it unless you want to." I was incredibly thankful when she stepped in as I was a bit nonplussed and was unclear about how I was going to respond. That left me the chance to say something like, "Please, I know all about Tinker or at least all I want to know. But, Ladies, please tell me about yourselves?"

With that Elaine began to explain that she was from Arizona. Phoenix actually. She had come to the area to attend Stanford, developed an interest in law, so here she was. Elaine and Sandra both knew each other at Stanford, but not well. However, when they got to Hastings and found each other in the same first year section, they became better friends, and in a matter of weeks, roommates. Tinker was in their first year section. When my face looked a bit puzzled, Elaine explained that the first year class at UC Hastings was 500. That was then divided into 5 sections of 100 students each and each of the sections took all of their first-year courses together since the entire 500 took the exact same courses, but taught by different law professors. Tinker was grinning. I could tell, going into the dinner, that he was fond of Elaine, but I sensed more than that. He seemed proud of her, almost as if he was showing her off.

In the moment's silence, Sandra told of growing up in San Francisco ("NEVER Frisco!") with a father who was a successful partner in a law firm in town and a mother who was a debutante and extremely active on the social scene. She said nothing about being a deb herself, but I quickly inferred that. She had gone to an San Francisco prep school and loved the City, as much as saying that she wanted to spend the rest of her life here.

Yet, she began to talk about making frequent travels to the world's exciting places. Sandra, who was tall and lovely, sounded, unintentionally to be sure, spoiled but nonetheless charming. From that point the evening moved forward; and, amid a few questions from me, the rest of the dinner and drinking was spent discussing the law, their school, Hastings, and the greater San Francisco Bay Area.

After Tinker and I paid the check, he asked if I would mind taking Sandra home as he and Elaine had an errand to run. I had trouble thinking of what errand they might run at this time of night, but agreed to see that Sandra got home. When we got in my Charger, I remember the first thing Sandra said, "Please call me Sandy. My parents hate it as a nickname. I'm not sure why they gave me the name." A pause, then, "Since I probably won't see you after your time here, I feel safe with you calling me that."

We drove less than a mile to her place on a narrow hilly street in an area called Russian Hill. I walked her to her door. She stood there long enough for me to know that I should kiss her. So, I did. She did not invite me in. We exchanged pleasant goodnights and I left.

3

THE INTERVIEWS

At shortly after 0800 on that Friday morning, I was seated in the Twelfth District Commander's conference room relatively down the table, but on the side opposite where each captain would sit for his questioning. CAPT Carlsen, Chief of CCGD12 Legal was to lead the questioning. Four civilians entered the room. One was from Texaco's legal department, the second was the Texaco tanker's captain, and the others were civilian lawyers from what turned out to be a firm in San Francisco and a firm in Houston. After introductions, CAPT Carlsen began the questioning by seeking to have the Texaco captain placed under oath. That idea was quickly rejected by his civilian lawyers who explained that this interview was so preliminary and the facts and data so unclear that they could not begin to prepare their client for a statement under oath. The most they would allow was to have the captain explain generally the course, times and personnel on duty at the time leading up to, but not immediately before, the course changes leading to the collision.

Consternation was given a voice by CAPT Carlsen, but to no avail. When the captain paused for breath, one of the 2 civilian lawyers quickly filled the sound gap by announcing that they had prepared a handout explaining the need for counsel for the captain, his rights and obligations, and what they saw as the law governing what the captain could be asked at this particular moment. I still have a copy of that document more than 40 years later. To me, it was the beginning of a lifelong quest to separate the callous concept of best legal outcome from real justice. Looking back now, with so many years of hindsight, I have begun to

appreciate how even the best of intentions can become compro-
mised, and those doing the most by way of compromise, justify
their behavior in the name of a quality legal representation in a
system built on the adversary precept, no matter the level and
degree of the ethics which get tortured in the process.

What followed was little more than what could be read in the
summary of the interviews undertaken by the USCG first re-
sponders on scene. If the captain were a prisoner of war, his
comments would have amounted to little more than name, rank
and serial number.

The afternoon session for the other captain was almost a car-
bon copy of what had transpired in the morning. Afterward, the
CG officers stayed at the conference table for a strategy conference. Investigative power was given to a number of those present by federal statute. The gathering of physical evidence in
virtually every form was allowed, some requiring more legal
power than just Coast Guard identification, included subpoenas
and the participation of a U.S. Attorney, if needed. The preser-
vation of documentary evidence was essential as was the need
to statementize the non-decision makers. And over the course
of an hour, I came to see that these Coast Guard leaders were
not willing to be put off by these civilian lawyers without ex-
hausting all of their available remedies, including the appear-
ance of a U.S. Attorney to participate.

As things began to wind down, I asked what would have fa-
cilitated a more thorough and timely investigation. To my surprise, led by CAPT Carlsen, these senior officers laid out the
need for federal legislation to control the construction of ships
carrying dangerous cargo, to protect the fragile shore side envi-
ronments through which these ships passed as they traversed
between ports, to set penalties for violations, and to allow the
investigating authorities broader jurisdiction and powers to
move quickly and secure evidence while it was fresh, including
recollections of those with potential responsibility. I took careful

notes for my return to Coast Guard Headquarters. This, together with the tragedy in San Juan Harbor just the year before as well as the increasing media coverage, helped to begin the process leading to the first federal Clean Water Act.

Together with the evenings spent with Tinker and his law school friends, this day's lessons stoked a curiosity in me of whether or not I might be cut out to be a lawyer, someone to help correct the injustices of the world like this giant oil spill contaminating San Francisco Bay, its shoreline, and injuring their inhabitants.

4

LAST 24 HOURS

The day of taking statements as well as all of my observations led me to believe that the two oil companies whose tankers were involved in the collision may have planned in advance for just such a catastrophe, not necessarily from the perspective of preventing a collision or containing and cleaning up afterward, but rather from the prospect of how to deal with the investigating authorities and the limits of those authorities' powers as well as their willingness to challenge highly reputed, seemingly well- prepared legal talent.

Although I held this opinion strongly, I was unwilling to reduce all of this to writing to protect the relatively innocent Coast Guards personnel who might be subject to unjustified criticism, especially if my report should find its way into the hands of a frustrated congressman looking for ready scapegoats for what was being called by the media the worst environmental spill and ensuing contamination of all time.

No one in San Francisco would see my report before the Chief of Operations/Search and Rescue (OSR) who had handed me this assignment by telephone and given me very specific instructions on the first person to receive my report. Reluctantly, I had two sets of photographs developed and copied my report. Against the possibility of a plane crash or the like, the copy would survive. Otherwise, Tinker, to whom I had entrusted these documents would see they were destroyed as soon as he heard that my report had been placed in the hands of CAPT Redman. This entrustment was accomplished as we spoke at his apartment while I was packing and he was changing for dinner.

He asked me to come along. Then, with a sheepish grin, he handed me a small box. I opened it. Perhaps a bit surprised, but not shocked, I found a diamond ring. As his best friend, he wanted me there. He explained Sandra would be there as well. I agreed.

We each drove to the Spinnaker, a Sausalito waterfront restaurant nestled between a marina full of sailboats and the Golden Gate Ferry terminal connecting with San Francisco. The ladies arrived using the ferry service and arrived a few minutes after Tinker and me.

Upon being seated, a bottle of MOET Champagne arrived as if by magic. Tinker made a short speech, then kneeling in front of Elaine in a room full of strangers he officially asked her the BIG Question. Of course, she said "Yes'" and the room broke into polite applause. Toasts followed. Mine had little preparation, but the other three had time to prepare and said things that were romantic, sentimental and spoke to a bright future of many years. The mood stayed celebratory for a multicourse meal. Someone sent a second bottle of champagne and a good time was generally had. Having to fly east early the next morning, I was ready to go before the others. Then, much to my surprise, Sandra asked if I would drive her home so that the newly affianced could have more time together. I agreed.

Outside their building, I had no problem finding a parking space. Before I could get out to go open Sandy's door, she reached over and pulled my face to hers. What followed was a long, lingering complex kiss. We stayed that way for a few minutes until as if by unspoken consent, we broke apart. I went around and opened Sandy's car door. We walked up to her apartment door hand-in-hand. She opened the door and turned to give me a final kiss, but first said, "I hope you find your way back to San Francisco, and not too long from now." We kissed and then she was gone.

Driving back across the Golden Gate Bridge to Tinker's

apartment in Sausalito, I began to put together my thoughts and feelings of the last few days. I arrived as Tinker was leaving to take Elaine home. I gave her a quick kiss, told Tinker I would try to see him in the a.m. if I was asleep when he returned. As I was about to turn away, Elaine left with a good-bye similar to that of Sandy. After quickly packing, I fell asleep considering options for my future. My family and life to date was in the East, but I had few strong connections there at the moment, except my mother, and I had begun to question whether the Coast Guard would provide me with the type of life I sensed that I wanted for myself. A potential new career course with different options was opening up for me. Should I risk this change and take it? The assessment was made within days of my return to Washington D.C.

5

LIFE-CHANGING DECISION

The days and weeks that followed my temporary duty (TDY) in the Twelfth Coast Guard District (CCGD 12) were some of my most tense since my return to the Mainland from my Hawaiian recovery following Viet Nam. On the return flight to D.C., I began to realize that not only was a decision needed on the course that my life would follow but that I needed to find out if I was even qualified to go to law school. A conversation with Tinker before my departure, and after swearing him to secrecy, gave me to understand that I would need to take the Law School Aptitude Test (LSAT) to learn about my actual readiness for admission. (Tinker told me that a score of 700 plus would be needed for out of state admission to a California state law school, like Hastings.) So, first things first, I found out when to take that test: February was last date in the Admissions cycle to be considering attendance starting in August. So, hesitation about taking the LSAT or to act to begin gathering other Admissions data would undermine my making a rational assessment about my future. Then, there was also the very real issue of where would I go, if and when I finally decided on law school.

I had written Thank You notes to Tinker and Elaine as well as Sandy. I even wrote a note to Carolyn. They all wrote back. Carolyn after a delay of more than a month. They all sounded welcoming. I failed to write anyone of them except Tinker after that.

Against this process weighed the Coast Guard's offer to have me integrate from being a reserve officer on active duty to the Regular Coast Guard. (Please understand that virtually all

Regular Coast Guard officers come from one of two sources: the Coast Guard Academy or they are prior enlisted personnel who either receive a direct commission or, in most cases, go through Officer Candidate School (OCS). People like me who have no prior Coast Guard career and go through OCS, receive a Reserve commission.) From a career perspective, a few of the Mustangs (prior enlisted) move very high up through the ranks, but the CAPT/ADM ranks are largely reserved for Coast Guard Academy grads. Still, with my career experience to date, especially Viet Nam (more later on that) and my two tours at USCG HQ, my chances of moving up appeared much better than the average integrating Reserve officer, Academy or not. On that end, it was incumbent to try to find out what types of assignments might await me if I accepted the offer to go Regular Coast Guard. So, while doing my job, I spent some time finding out who would be the right detailer to ask about possible assignments (not to mention my current reporting officer).

Then, there was the last, and no doubt the biggest, issue: Family! On the one hand, I had been on the move so much that I had not formed any strong relationship with a woman. But if I did, family would have a role in that. Still, the biggest factor would be my mother. Kate O'Neill had a husband go off to war, and come back: now, she had a son. The husband never really left her again. What about the son? Could I do that? Should I do that? These were all factors which needed to be resolved-now!

1.

The LSAT was an event for which I undertook no real preparation. In high school, I took the SATs without special studies. In OCS, I took the Graduate Record with no preparation. Both had resulted in high 700s and an 800 in math in high school. The only real issue was the person sitting next to me in the exam. He folded his test booklet in half and would flop it back and forth, making distracting noises. At the first break I asked him to stop making the noise. He said, "Mind your own business," in a dismissive manner. I leaned toward him and whispered, "I asked nicely. If you make one more annoying noise with your test booklet, I will see you at the next break and IT will not happen again!" He stayed quiet.

I got my LSAT result in 3 Weeks: 752. So much for qualifying. Meanwhile, I had sent for about 15 -20 applications. Some were expensive. Harvard and Stanford were $100. I had bought 2 books at Tinker's suggestion which evaluated law schools. I settled on applying to 7. One of them was Hastings. The application process was necessary before deciding on California. George Washington, University of Maryland (my home state), Penn, and Harvard were all in the East. Any of them would resolve the family issue.

Stanford, Boalt Hall (UC-Berkeley) and Hastings (UC-San Francisco) would all raise the family issue. My undergraduate grade point average was a bit of a wild card. Since I played sports and was socially active, not to mention a level of disdain I developed for some of the required philosophy courses, left my GPA around 3.3 (out of a real 4.0 in those days) at Georgetown. The application process was a grind, but I got most of it done while awaiting the LSAT results. So, part one of the plan was underway.

2.

The detailer who would, in all likelihood, provide my first assignment, was LCDR Williams, a Mustang (this last point surprised me). I asked my boss, CDR Woods, who was a driving force in my getting integrated, if he thought I could talk to the detailer about what might come next. He responded by getting me an appointment. LCDR Williams was older than I expected, probably in his early to mid-40's. He was a straight shooter.

After a short introductory chat, he explained that the career path of a regular usually followed either sea service, air service or a profession (very few of this last group). I was not a pilot-type and had not disclosed law school, so that left me telling him that I would be going down the sea service route, which I thought would work well for my first assignment with my experience in Viet Nam as an XO, and then, ever so briefly, CO. Was I wrong? You bet.

I had forgotten one of the first rules of military machinations: if something can be done either the hard way or the easy way, it generally gets done the hard way. Integration was apparently no exception. Academy types who would do sea service had their first assignment on a "Big White One." This did not mean Moby Dick. In the USCG, it meant a high endurance cutter (WHEC), or maybe an icebreaker (WAGB) for 18 -24 months.

The next assignment would often be a command; a small cutter, like a 95-footer, or a Loran Station, isolated duty with 15 -20 enlisted. In both instances, there would be chief petty officer (CPO) or First class to act as an interface with the crew. As a result, my time in Coast Guard HQ as well as my time in Viet Nam were anomalies relative to a regular career path. So, because I would soon be promoted to 0-3, Lieutenant (LT), I would be too senior for a WHEC first assignment, and that left only a WAGB, with its very large crew complement, to make the needed career course correction to get me on the road to long term success as a regular Coast Guard officer. We then talked about the WAGB fleet and their types of cruises. I would be facing a minimum assignment of 18, and more likely 24, months with a minimum of 2 deployments on an icebreaker. I asked about other options. He said I could request whatever I wanted, but what he had told me was what I would probably get (integration carried a minimum 36 month extension of active duty by contract.).

A conversation with CDR Woods, a pilot, essentially confirmed what detailer Williams had told me. My boss tried to persuade me by telling me about his one deployment as a chopper pilot on the USCGC Glacier on a 6 month cruise to Antarctica. But his duties began and ended with his aircraft and covered "only 6 months." I began to have serious doubts about integration. I had been aboard the Glacier in Long Beach about 24 months ago on a TDY assignment during my first tour at USCG HQ. It was a different Coast Guard than what I knew. My doubts deepened.

3.

Finally, I was faced with what I had known all along would be the hardest decision: whether or not I could bring myself to leave the Northeast Corridor and relocate to California for a minimum of 3 years. My primary concern was my mother, Kate O'Neill, who was an enormously strong woman, had her life shaken to its roots in the last few years.

When I went into the Coast Guard, she thought I would be safe from the dangers of Viet Nam. She had already endured the very war long absences of my father with but a single visit in almost six years. She had come to know more than she should have about my father's harrowing brushes with death during the early years of the war; and then, the prolonged absence of his time in and about London, England and later France. (She never said anything, but those were some of the best years of her life, she was without her man and missing him terribly. His letters said the same, she told us, but as the years went by, I came to believe that she was concerned that all of the years could force him to be unfaithful.)

His return, two more daughters, his successful insurance agency, and her dedication as an active mother and mentor to her daughters and who doted on her only son, were the essence of a happy middle life. She did not miss her politics (more later). She went to Philadelphia often to see her family. Her father's health began to fail, as did that of both of my Dad's parents. My older sister went off to college and we all began to sense that this was the beginning of a new stage in our lives. My father's counsel was always: let them go off to college or follow their dreams, that will always lead them back to us as their parents. My staying in the D.C. area to attend Georgetown, not only as a second generation legacy but also because I possessed an uncanny ability to put a fairly large bouncy ball through a ten foot high hoop from a distance of 15 - 20 feet, had buffered my aging for four years as my sisters approached college age. But then came Viet Nam and the draft.

In those days. A single man, about to lose his college deferment was subject to being drafted in 60 - 90 days. As a result, my father worked his connections and was able to get me an interview for Coast Guard OCS while I was still in the second semester of my senior year of college. Everything went well and I was sworn in before graduation. OCS began in mid- September 1966. This meant I had a minimum commitment through January 1970. My father was proud and my mother was elated, I would not be in the ground war that was the Viet Nam of the evening news every night.

My Coast Guard tour was perfect as I was stationed at USCG HQ on Pennsylvania Avenue. Then, in a matter of a few months, we learned that the Coast Guard would be sending 30 of its 82' patrol boats to Viet Nam for riverine/coastal patrol and arms smuggling interdiction.

That required 60 junior officers. I eventually became one of them. Everything began to change in our lives. (This is not the place to discuss my 21 months leading up to, in, and returning from 'Nam. More on that later.) Before Christmas 1967, we began patrols along the Mekong Delta.

Almost a year into the 13 month tour, there was a major Viet Cong offensive with various news blackouts. Letter transmittal became difficult. My parents were concerned and my father had been losing his appetite. While I was out of communication, dad had what appeared to be a minor stroke. Many tests were run. Finally, a provisional diagnosis of some form of liver cancer was reached. The doctors wanted to do surgery right away to understand the extent and to better understand what was happening. Mom and Dad agreed. I knew nothing. The surgery was a disaster: not that it went wrong, but instead it was what they found - multiple tumors in the liver and the pancreas was almost totally consumed by the carcinoma. The doctors gave him 2- 3 weeks to live. He didn't last two. My sisters were devastated. My mother was heartbroken. All the while, she was worried sick because her son seemed to have disappeared. (Again, more later.)

From that series of events to this point of decision had been an extraordinarily difficult period for my mother, but she had made scores of adjustments and my being brought back to USCG HQ had made her life that much better. I could not decide what to do, so I finally concluded that the best course was to talk the decision through with her.

4.

More than 30 years ago, I first began to reconsider and *present feedback on my mother* and *my decision. Dr. Arnaud preserved several transcripts of sessions where we discussed this meeting exhaustively. What follows is my thoughts* and *memories of that day, and what lay behind some of the remarks* and *the outcomes:*

My mother, whom I shall call Kate (although I would never address her as that) was home when I came in early in the evening from my day at USCG HQ. The family home in Chevy Chase, MD was empty. My 2 younger sisters were extremely socially and athletically active, thus, rarely home before 7 p.m. Kate was in the kitchen preparing food for a bar-b-que, a family tradition when the weather began to turn pleasant in the short D.C. area Spring. She asked if I would bar-b-que the chicken.

It had been my father's task my entire life until I returned from Viet Nam and he was no longer there. I am certain she was expecting nothing more than an assent on my part, which I gave readily.

But then, I quickly suggested we have a cocktail and asked if we could have a chat as I had something important to talk to her about. Kate agreed. Somehow, she seemed a bit nervous as I made a small pitcher of vodka martinis. We moved to the patio outside our kitchen and family room and took seats under the blossoming elms and oaks which dominated the rolling hillocks just north of D.C.

We sat silently for a few moments, sipped our drinks and silently toasted my missing father/her husband, and who had loved his Vodka Martinis. When I broke the silence, I immediately broached the subject of law school. I did it by reviewing the options currently pending in my life. Kate nodded in an understanding motherly fashion. I felt we started off on the same page. I had given this "chat" a good deal of thought. When I paused she readily agreed that law school seemed like a good idea. Also, she seemed relieved as she added that she had several offers to consider for my father's independent insurance agency. That if I wanted to follow that path, it would make her life far easier by allowing her to move forward with a sensible plan to realize the full benefit of her husband's independent agency which he had created from an idea and hard work between 1946 and his death less than a year ago. She seemed to think that this presentation was over.

When I started to go into the law schools to which I had applied, she nodded at each East Coast name. Then I said Stanford and she sat up straighter in her chair. When I said Hastings it was as if she had never heard the name. Then I told her it was the school where Tinker went and I had told her about it when I got back from San Francisco a couple of months ago. She looked at me harder and said, "You're looking for an adventure.

A clean break with your life here. Was it something in Viet Nam? Something about going to war?" (I was not sure how to reply from the way she phrased the question. As I sat in those sessions that are the basis for this recall, I did not know the answer. As I sit here today writing this, I think I do know, but am not certain enough to say so at this point in this narrative.)

Then, she continued as though those questions were rhetorical, and perhaps they were. Instead she said, "Have you thought about moving to the other side of the country and what it would mean in your life? Have you thought about what a degree from a West Coast law school would mean if you move back here to practice?" These were the questions for which I had prepared and my answers seemed to calm her.

But then she asked the one question that I knew would be coming, but I wasn't that sure that she would buy my answer. "Why do you need to go all the way to California?"

My response, "You know I was in Long Beach briefly when we were shipping over to 'Nam, and even more briefly when I went out to tour the Glacier to get a sense of Allowance Lists as it is the biggest cutter in the Guard. Those were my only taste of California and al I saw were freeways and the same US Navy Base on both stints. It was warm, sort of interesting, bustling and I had a lot to do and not much time to explore. But my trip a few months back to San Francisco was different. I was busy, but I still had some time to see things. Tinker was there and he served as a bit of a guide. I met interesting people. The area was gorgeous. And I found myself getting very interested in law school. As much as I think you want me to take over Dad's insurance business, it's just not quite right for me. Besides, if it turns out to be a mistake, or the wrong place, assuming I even get into a California school, I can always come home and either finish up here, or try something different. After all, I am not getting any younger."

Kate seemed to understand that what I was considering was a life not unlike what she and my Dad had created in greater

D.C. as a young couple from Philadelphia, which must have seemed an adventure to them coming on the heels of the Great Depression. The real differences were the sheer distance and I had no Kate to take with me.

Still, she seemed satisfied with my answers. She even offered to help with my expenses. Then, for moments, her focus seemed to drift away. I was uncertain that this had been the right thing to do to her at this still difficult time in her life. But my own needs were such that I convinced myself then that it needed to be done, and done so that I knew what course I would plot when I began to hear back from the law schools.

When she drifted back to me, she said, "There are airplanes now. You won't be that far away. Besides, once Meaghan and Mary Rose are off to college, this house will begin to feel empty and I will need to make some decisions."

That was my end of my fretting for then. My mother had made the decision for me. If I got into a California law school, I would go to one in the San Francisco area.

A Subtle Explanation

All of the recitals that follow are summaries of what I said, heard, and thought sometimes long before the events of latter 1975 giving rise to my relationship with Dr. Arnaud. The words are mine as I create this recollection and in most cases but represent my very best recollection of what occurred long ago, some memories including a few words that have stayed with me for years - all superimposed with more than 40 years of life experience which no doubt changed some of my thoughts and many of my feelings.

To better understand all that came next and in the ensuing years, it will prove helpful to explain my family and my life leading up to that trip to San Francisco. What follows may appear random at times, but please realize that this is a product of more than 35 years of psychoanalysis superimposed on my sometimes chaotic life and the lives of some of those which have touched mine for better, worse, or both!

6

MY FAMILY — MY FATHER

My father was borne Robert Emmett Joseph Charles O'Neill in Germantown, a section of Philadelphia, in 1915. His parents were 2d generation Irish who had met in Baltimore while in school, fell in love young, married against her parents' wishes, and as a result, had migrated to Philadelphia for the better job market. My grandfather was a bricklayer, a very good one, and spent the greater part of his life working for John B. Kelly Brick Company of Philadelphia. My father was the third of seven children, five of whom reached adulthood. Because of his skill and the need for war critical construction, my grandfather, Liam, was not called to serve in the First Great War, something he seemed to regret greatly in his later years. He lost one of his older brothers in the Ardennes. Two others were injured, though both recovered without any significant disability. As a result of this family experience, when the time came, military obligation would play a central role in our family's lives.

My paternal grandmother was an energetic, sometimes despotic, worker with a heart of gold. To supplement her husband's income which was not insignificant for the time, they had purchased a corner store selling a variety of general merchandise needed by their neighbors, especially the type that would not alone mandate a shopping trip to the grocery store some distance away. My grandparents lived in a house constructed of Kelly brick-three stories high with a basement and adjacent neighbors on either side — it was a typical big city row house of the time and housed the family of seven in a degree of comfort, though that would be doubtful in this day and age. The key products of the store were milk, bread, fruit and ice cream, which was served in 4 flavors from behind the counter. The family, with the exception of my grandfather ran and staffed that store until all of the children were off to college or to their adult lives. That store provided a wonderful foundation for getting on in life in general and provided very real values of punctuality, hard work, dedication and how to treat your fellow man. My father spoke of that store often. Surely, it was a central point in his formative life.

After 3 years of high school at St. Thomas Moore, my father concluded that he would like to go to college. His oldest brother was a bricklayer for Kelly. His older sister was an operator for Pennsylvania Bell, an AT&T company. Neither had given higher education a serious thought. Robert Emmett was different. He always would be. He decided, with help from Brother Francis, a mentor at his high school, that he should go Georgetown College in Washington, D.C. However, the Great Depression was in full swing and his father was not working full time, the store was doing only OK, and his savings were not that great.

Emmett, as his family called him, set to work on the first great challenge of his life. When my father first approached his father and mother (who appeared to actually control the family purse strings) about the concept of continuing his formal education, it was with some trepidation as he knew he would need their financial assistance. However, he had a plan. He often spoke of his schooling and how much he appreciated going to St. Thomas Moore, also how he appreciated being able to take a pre-college curriculum, including Latin, Greek, English literature, some higher math, and even a couple of science courses. (In those days, there was no terminology for college prep courses as this was considered a liberal arts course of the Catholic variety.) He had hoped that this approach would allow them to be the ones to first broach the concept of his going on to college. It did not.

When this first prong of his plan failed, he was ready with the second ploy: raise college, but not Georgetown. As he prepared to return for his last year of high school having spent the summer as a lifeguard at a local municipal pool, he encountered his parents together with no other siblings around - a rarity . He gathered his wits and went ahead and told them about his plan to go on to college. He was shocked by first his father's response, "Why would you ever consider not going on to college?" And more so by his mother's, "Why do you think we spent all that money sending you to St. Tommy's?"

He recovered quickly and got their assurance that they saw him going onward (and to his dismay they mentioned one of his younger sisters as well). Feeling optimistic in light of their responses and the positively charged atmosphere, he then proffered his plan for Georgetown. That proved too much. Way too much!!! Shaking their heads, "No," one said LaSalle, while the other muttered Villanova. Both considered, and by virtue of his settling upon Georgetown, rejected by both. Now, came his first critical decision—-press the issue or thank his parents for their positive attitude and withdraw the choice of college for another day. Realizing they had not agreed on a choice for him, he quickly chose the second path —- with the thought that he might change their minds in the months before the application process began.

***

My father succeeded. He matriculated at Georgetown University and graduated with a degree in English Literature while looking forward to a career as a school teacher. Still the Depression persisted and schools were not hiring. He tried writing, but could get nothing published. He was despondent. Also, he was in love.

Mary Catherine Garrity went to Dominican College in

Washington, D.C. She was beautiful, smart and very selective. In the Fall of his junior year, he went to one of her school's mixers (as they were called then). Some of his friends had been before. Emmett had not. Some of his friends knew some of her friends and asked them to dance with each other. He stood with her alone for moments, then said, "I would really like to ask you to dance." And before he could finish the slowly spaced sentence, she inserted, "Well, please do so." To which he finished his sentence, "But I don't know how." An awkward moment ensued. He stared down. But then she grabbed his hand and said, "We shall go over there where none of our friends can see, and I shall teach you in a jiffy." They did and she did. When the song ended, they stayed where they were. In a few songs, Emmett had the hang of it. As they began to go back to the others, she asked his name and he gave it all, but ended with, "My family calls me Emmett."

She responded that her full name was Mary Catherine Rose Mary Garrity, but, "I call myself Kate. Do you mind if I call you Robert?" And that was the beginning. There were some hiccups, other young men. And then, there was her family. As it turned out, Kate's family home was only a few miles from Robert's, only a few miles apart in the older northwestern section of Philadelphia. But there lay the problem. As Philadelphia had evolved into a morass of little sections that were each like its own small town, each with its own peoples, social scale and attitudes. Germantown was then a higher end blue collar with types like the O'Neill's. Its next western neighbor, Mt. Airy was where the white collar types had come to evolve and included small business owners and managers, and some professional types. By early 1937, few remained who had not been touched deeply by the Depression. The western most section was one of the highest echelons of Philadelphia north of The Main Line, Chestnut Hill, home to people of wealth and privilege including many successful professionals, and older Philadelphia families.

Kate was from Chestnut Hill and her parents had spent years securing their place in that "town."

On a trip home, he met her parents. They were pleasant and polite, but not overly forthcoming. Dinner conversation appeared a bit strained between Kate, her parents, and siblings. A few questions about his future were asked. His response about teaching English Literature failed to raise any rejoinder at all. When he left, Kate apologized and said she would see him on the train back to D.C.

She did not show up for the train or call his family home. She had the number. That night he tried her dorm, only to be told she was not there. Two days passed. Two calls. No Kate. Finally, he took streetcars and made his way to her campus. He saw her heading back to her dormitory after class and called to her. She looked at him for a long second, covered her eyes with one hand, and broke into a run. He caught up to her quickly, then said only, "Kate." She stopped. Her eyes met his. Her eyes were red, very red, more than a few tears red. He reached out to her. She froze. Seconds passed. Then, she was in his arms.

***

So, their relationship proceeded without the support of Kate's family. She would be a year later graduating from college. With no job prospects for teaching in D.C., and none in Philadelphia for that matter, they seemed doomed when Kate had to return to Washington for her senior year. With no clear source of a self-sustaining income, Robert even turned to applying for sales positions. With no experience, he could not get this work either. His parents, who liked Kate but were unsure if she would stand by him in a long distance relationship, were also concerned— more for their Emmett.

Happenstance intervened one afternoon. Robert's dad was working on a job in the developing northeastern Philadelphia when John B. Kelly, Sr., himself, came to the jobsite. Without any notice he walked up to his bricklayer of many years asking, "O 'Neill, how're you doing these days?"

The father replied without much thought, "Considering how you have kept me busy all these years, Mr. Kelly, I can say nothing bad. My only real concern at the moment is my son, Emmett, who graduated from Georgetown last June, cannot get a job in Washington, and his girlfriend who goes to Dominican, returns for her last year in a few weeks. The wife and I are feeling very badly for him as he thinks he's in love." Then, realizing he had overstepped himself, he began to apologize, but Kelly stopped him saying, "I understand O'Neill. I have children. Meg's married, Robert, Jr. hasn't found anyone, and young Grace, well, she thinks she wants to go into acting rather than college when her time comes. Thankfully, that's a few years away. Parents need to be concerned for their children. If not us, who?"

Dad said that Granddad was so nonplussed by John B's response that he was at a complete loss for words. "But listen," the senior Kelly continued, "The reason I wanted to see you is I think a great deal of your work. We are going to expand our home on Henry Avenue and I would like you to do the brick work. OK?" Robert's father agreed readily, and John B. Kelly left with no further discussion. Thus, it came as a great surprise some weeks later when Congressman Tim Burke's office called the O'Neill home and asked to speak to Robert Emmett. He was home and took the call. When he turned to face his mother, he was smiling, but near tears, but got out, "I was just offered a job in Congressman Burke's office in D.C. for a year. I cannot believe it. How did this happen?" His mother, ever practical, asked, "Did you take it?" But he was already calling Kate!

When his father came home that night, Emmett told him what had happened. With a smile, his father said, "Sounds like one Irishman decided to help another's son," and went on to describe what had been said on his jobsite the few days before.

***

*This section, including what has come before this notation as will
be any number thot follow, is pieced together from Doctor Arnaud's
interview notes, or in later days, from her tapes of interviews. Many
sessions rambled and covered multiple topics. My parents had a pro-
found impact on me. Some background about my mother, also, of necessity, must be included in capturing my view of my father. Many of
the quoted statements are as accurate as I can make them. Most were
the subject of dinner conversations with my parents and some with
my grandparents when I was quite young.*

***

So, my parents saw even more of each other than they had
the last two years. They knew what confronted them. Kate could
perhaps go onto another year or two of education, but Robert
knew he had to get on with his life. He also knew that this job
would end on 30 June 1938. He would need to line up something
new before then, or move back with his parents yet again. They
began to talk marriage. Robert was concerned that he could not
begin to provide Kate with the life she had enjoyed as her par-
ent's daughter. When he finally told her that, in words like those,
Kate looked at him, paused for a few moments and broke into a
laugh. Kate had a sense of humor, but was not given to frivolity.
Robert began to back away, but she reached for his hands, and
looking into his eyes, said, "Why would you ever think I would
care about money? Or our lifestyle? How could I be worried? If
we are together, I think we will find a way to do whatever needs
to be done." Moments later, he proposed marriage and she accepted without hesitation.

***

Kate's parents took the news poorly, with reservations and quite a few recriminations, but ultimately they acquiesced. When it came to the wedding itself, it appeared they were going to hold back. When the mothers met to discuss the groom's family's proposed guest list, Robert's mother asked if they could contribute to invite another dozen guest. Kate's mother seemed disturbed, but did not respond immediately. Mrs. O'Neill went on to explain that they wanted to invite the Kelly's because of their long working history. Nancy Garrity was taken a bit aback. (Some Philadelphians viewed the Kelly's as "serious social climbers." Many Main Line Philadelphians viewed the Irish as a race as close to being "criminals.".) Nancy said she would speak with her husband. Two days later, the Garrity's agreed to expand the O'Neill list by 12 invitees without charge. All of the O'Neill's and Kate believed that John B's political clout in Philadelphia politics was the deciding factor, if not having Congressman Burke on the Groom's guest list. Because of the two families different home sections, Chestnut Hill did not seem the best choice for the wedding. Instead, Robert and Kate were married at the Philadelphia Irish Center City parish of St. Michael's with the reception across Rittenhouse Square at the Barclay Hotel.

***

My father continued his job with Congressman Burke. My mother, having a superior education, was accepted into a training program with the Chesapeake Bell Telephone Co. (This meant that she mostly skipped working as an operator and some other positions, but to her surprise her training program required her to be proficient in all of the operating skills of the company that were then considered " women's work.") With both of them working, the couple found a nice place to live just off Connecticut Avenue from which they could walk to work on nice days and they also had convenient public transportation. Best of all, with the monetary presents from their wedding and some careful money management by early 1940, they had somewhat significant savings—enough that they considered their first child. With little effort, Kate was pregnant by the beginning of 1941. Still, there were great concerns: the war in Europe was going poorly for the freedom loving countries of Western Europe —- only Churchill and Great Britain, aided by her Commonwealth of Nations, stood between Hitler and the Nazis complete domination of Europe (My parents detested Stalin and the Communists so they gave little recognition to Stalin's Soviet forces and the Eastern Front—-the same was true for Mussolini and Italy which seemed to have virtually no role in the Axis' successes.).

As that war pressed on to what seemed an imminent Nazi victory, my parents, like many million Americans, became concerned about what would follow that putative Nazi total victory. They reached a conclusion that would change the balance of their lives —- my father joined the U.S. Navy. It was to some extent an act of patriotism, but they saw it as being prepared for a war that would someday, perhaps soon, involve the United States.

After all, President Roosevelt, in what had become a highly charged political drama had begun to give or sell as much aid as possible to Great Britain. Congressman Burke agreed with Tim's decision and he interceded to see that my Dad got into one of the first Navy officer candidate schools (OCS). In the same timeframe, they became the parents of Rose Mary Ellen O'Neill.

So, it was at the beginning of 1941 that my father shipped off to OCS in Portsmouth, Virginia. My mother stayed on in D.C. still holding her job. Both sets of grandparents begged her to return to Philadelphia. But when they explained that they wanted to see where Dad would be stationed before reaching any decision on that move, they all acquiesced and became more frequent visitors to see their granddaughter, the redoubtable Rose Mary.

***

As you can see above, I could not explain my father without including my mother. They always seemed a pair functioning as one. At some point, we shall return to my father, but now we need to try to begin to understand my mother. As you can see she was not co-dependent. After all, she is one of the major obstacles to my going to California——perhaps the biggest.

7

MY FAMILY—MY MOTHER

Kate Garrity O'Neill as she was always known during my lifetime was at her core a force of nature. Irish families recognize her type and call each a matriarch. Mary Katherine, "Kate," O'Neill was so much more than that. Left alone with a baby and a job (and my father having taken a serious pay cut to join the Navy), Kate quickly began to rally with many of her friends from college who lived in D.C. Some were married. Two had children and one of them had a job as well. Many of her friends, but not all, were employed. Almost universally they believed war was inevitable. Using this dynamic, with Kate as one of the leaders, they set about organizing themselves, adding others, and came up with a unified group which would provide an early form of daycare as well as supplying training to get into the job market and to gather job availabilities. They became the Dominican Women's Action Committee of Washington, D.C. (but they were open to others as well and their ranks swelled.).

I cannot explain my mother, I can only tell you about her from my own experiences as well as stories about her from Rose Mary, some of her siblings, my grandparents, and a few other Garritys. When born, she was a beautiful baby (her mother Nancy was very pretty as a young woman and she aged very well). She began to talk at 10 months, she cut her teeth with minimal pain, walked at 13 months and all of the other functions were well ahead of schedule as well. She was beautiful, athletic, intelligent, social, and above all from an early age, fiercely independent. She went through her schooling excelling in all phases.

She dated, but never found a Mr. Right until my father. Why she chose him was never clear. And, I never had the ability to ask her that kind of direct question. Rose Mary has no memory of those early days or of the War Years at all. The grandparents were in Philadelphia. So, I have what I could glean.

My father was stationed at the Norfolk Naval Base, home of the Atlantic Fleet. Once commissioned, he became a deck officer and watch stander on a destroyer. He went to sea starting in 1940, on convoy duty, guarding the U.S. Merchant Marine ships that were carrying critical goods to the United Kingdom - goods purchased by the British under Lend Lease (President Roosevelt could not give the British aid as we know it today because both houses of congress were under the control of fierce isolationists). Toward the beginning of 1941, the German U-boats began to attack the American flag ships in these convoys. (The Battle of Britain had not gone as well as the Nazis had planned and this risky process was one of several missteps which they made in these trying times-not the least of which was their decision to invade Russia - their treaty ally!)

After 2 trips across the Atlantic, my father got a week's leave. This was to be the last time for almost two years that my parents would be together. My father made LTJG and was the assistant navigator on his destroyer, the Clarke. When he returned, the convoy set sail, not for the British Isles, but the Russian northern port of Murmansk. (The U.S. was now beginning to supply materials to Russia.) While still north of Scotland, the Japanese bombed Pearl Harbor. Within days, a state of war existed between the U.S. and the Axis powers (Japan, Germany and Italy-they also controlled a good many vassal countries by virtue of preexisting victories).

The voyage ended safely. A brief stop was made at the royal Navy Base at Portsmouth, and the Clarke returned with a barely laden convoy to Boston and then New York. A new convoy was made up. My father was promoted to Lieutenant (LT) and became the navigator on the Clarke. He spoke with my mother but time did not permit leave. The United Sates was now fully at war.

Days after my father left for Murmansk again (my mother did not know where he had been or where he was going-security was very real: "Loose lips sink ships" seemed to have actual meaning in those early days when the U-boats dominated the shipping lanes of the North Atlantic), my mother got a call from Congressman Burke's office. With so many men off to serve, she was asked to fill my father's spot in that office. She accepted. Thus, began her career in government service.

While my father was off on convoy duty on the North Atlantic, my mother was becoming indispensable in the congressman's office. By 1942, Kate O'Neill was Congressman Burke's chief of staff. Weeks after being re-elected, the congressman accepted a direct commission as a Lieutenant Commander (LCDR) in the Navy. He asked the President to appoint his chief of staff to fill his post while he served his country. My mother became Congresswoman O'Neill.

My father was in awe when he was home on medical leave for 5 weeks toward year end 1942. He returned as a LCDR to the USS Baltimore, a heavy cruiser, as its communications officer in March of 1943. When he left my mother, he did not know she was pregnant which would result in our deferred meeting until after my birth. My mother with assistance from the grandmothers from time-to-time carried out her duties and gave birth without skipping a beat. Now, as the Pennsylvania representative from the district which encompassed her parents' home as well as that of her in-laws, she saw more of those families. Whatever rifts had occurred in the past were healed. My Dad was in harm's way and nothing but positive things could be said about him and his children. As for my mother, she would spend countless hours seeing to the varied needs of her constituency, however possible. In D.C., she would fulfill all of her duties, care for her 2 children, and still find time for her women's alliance and her many friends.

In June of 1944. The Allies landed in France at Normandy and a sense swept the Land that this war was now winnable. In November, the Allies were moving inexorably, albeit slowly, toward the Rhine and the German homeland. Paris was free. My mother was elected to fill the continuing term of Congressman Burke.

Now you may see why I described her as "a force of nature."

8

MY FATHER—AT WAR

Not until I was 10 and learning to sail did my father tell me about his first ship, the Clarke, being torpedoed. His story was matter of fact. Its purpose was to make me unafraid of the water, especially where the water was deep and we were not that close to land. He almost never spoke about his experiences in battle.

While crossing the North Atlantic, the U.S. Navy destroyers and other escort ships attempted to form a protective antisubmarine screen around the convoy of merchant ships and the battle cruisers which were in the forefront and rear of the formation to provide protection against surface raiders. The Clarke was on the southern flank of the convoy about mid-point in its formation. Early morning light was just appearing when the explosion occurred. There was no warning at all. My father was standing officer of the deck (OOD) watch at that moment. The explosion opened a massive hole in the Clarke's amidship, just aft of the bridge. Communications began to fail. The Commanding Officer (CO)'s cabin was aft of the bridge. When the CO did not come onto the bridge in less than a minute, Dad sent an enlisted watch stander to check on the CO. In seconds, he was back and reported that the CO had taken shrapnel in his legs and was not ambulatory: and, he sent orders, "Mr. O'Neill, carry on. Abandon ship, if necessary." That was all. The Executive Officer (XO)'s cabin was aft of the CO, It was largely destroyed.

The Clarke quickly began to list to starboard. The Damage Control officer, a warrant boatswain, reported to the bridge that the Clarke's hull had sustained a multi-deck hole incapable of being repaired and that the ship was taking on water at a fatal rate. Dad turned to the Quartermaster of the Watch (QOW) and ordered the "Abandon Ship" be sounded on the ship's claxon. He ordered the duty radioman to communicate the ship's condition to the Flotilla CO. At that point, he ordered all hands on the bridge to begin the rapid process of clearing the area of the ship before it went down. (Although not that big by warship standards, the Clarke was sufficiently large enough to take down swimmers close to its hull by the suction created when it went under.) My father then went to the CO's cabin. CDR Emerson was bleeding profusely from both legs. His face was ashen. He looked at my father and said, "Save yourself O'Neill. God go with you! That's all, MISTER." With that he looked away and my father backed onto the bridge. The Clarke's list had worsened seriously in the seconds he had been in the CO's cabin and Dad realized the destroyer could well capsize. With that, he went to the rail, removed his shoes, looked down at the lightening water which was now below the bridge rail as the ship continued to list into its fatal capsizing and jumped feet first about 15- 20 feet into the 40 degree water.

The shock of the cold was disconcerting, almost devastating, but his survival instinct was strong. He began to swim away from the ship's hull which was beginning to rotate and slope forward as the Clarke began its final throes of sinking. After what seemed like long minutes, a boat pulled toward him. He heard familiar voices. He saw familiar faces. The warrant boatswain and one of the deck hands pulled him from the sea. He felt almost frozen. They told him he had only been in the water 5 to 10 minutes. They had stood far enough away from the Clarke to avoid being dragged under, but close enough to pick up survivors. He was the only one plucked from the water that day.

They began to row in the direction of the convoy, hoping against hope that an outlying ship would see them. As the convoy began to move away, multiple explosions happened among the merchant ships. Chaos seemed to ensue. Destroyers began to break away to search for the culprit. Ships began to change to more evasive individual courses. The convoy began to lose formation. Then, suddenly, from behind came the sound of a megaphone, "Ahoy, down there. Come up the ladder just aft. If you need a hand tell us now." The CGC Spencer pulled them aboard.

Later that day, the nine Clarke survivors went up the rope ladder which was dropped down the hull of the cruiser Baltimore. All of this activity amid the chaos of the submarine attack left my father badly shaken. He was taken to the battle medical operations area deep in the bowels of the more heavily armored cruiser. Others from the life boat were there as well, but they deferred treatment to my father because he was the only one who had gone into the water. The LCDR doctor checked his vital signs, his wet clothing was taken off and he was provided with warm blankets and told to lay down. He did as instructed and feeling began to return to his arms and legs; then minutes later, to his feet and hands. My father knew before he jumped that his life expectancy in that water was no more than 20, maybe 30, minutes at most. He said he prayed when he jumped. I asked him what he thought about while he was in the water. I shall never forget his response, "Your mother. She was all I thought about. She was my whole life in what might have been my last moments. It was as if her image kept me moving in that paralyzingly cold water. Now back to your dealing with deep water. You'll see it will present little problem once you adjust to it. Go ahead. Jump in!"

***

On another occasion, while we were sailing, his years away during the war came up. I still remember him telling me how he, along with so many of those in the war far from home, measured time: by trying to conjure when they thought they might see home again. He also explained that many of those citizen soldiers drawn into the war felt that it was courting bad fortune to even consider with any degree of certainty that they would be going home. These pessimists believed the better course was to live one day at a time rather than to give voice to what might prove a long range, or impossible, objective — being home again.

Following his leave in late 1942, which gave rise to me, always unsaid, he was detailed as the permanent Navigation officer aboard the Baltimore. Promotions were happening quickly for those with sea experience and my father was no exception. He was now a LCDR and the fourth most senior officer on a ship with a battle complement of more than 500. When the Baltimore departed Norfolk in early 1943, it was not destined to return to U.S. waters for almost 3 years. She proceeded in an uneventful convoy to Portsmouth, England. There, she joined other battle-ready ships and troop carriers. They proceeded to North Africa and supported multiple landings. The Italian fleet was destroyed by the British in a battle near Malta, so the two great remaining dangers were Nazi air power and its U-boats. At the same time, the Russian front was taking more of the Nazi air power to stem the ever growing Russian armies defending their homeland; and, unknown to most of the Allied Navies, sonar and improved anti-submersible weaponry were taking an ever higher toll on the U-boats. My father's actual combat in the Mediterranean consisted almost entirely of repelling sporadic Luftwaffe attacks and supporting landings as the Allies began to sweep to victory in North Africa.

Months went by and the Baltimore was part of a small fleet that supported Allied landings on Sicily. A swift victory led to further landings on the Italian mainland at Anzio. The German Wehrmacht began to see that Allied victories in the southwest and Russian victories on the eastern front were beginning to forecast an unsuccessful end for the Nazi regime. That said, the

Germans fought ever harder while the Italians deposed their leader Mussolini and surrendered unceremoniously, and unconditionally, to the Allies. The Italian soldiers tried mightily to always surrender to Americans. They knew that many U.S. troops were from Italy not that many generations ago. Again, the Baltimore's role seemed secondary and supportive.

The Allied staff in London, now lead by an American General named Eisenhower was heavy on Army and Army Air Force staff, but light on Naval support personnel. Among those selected was Congressman, now CAPT Burke, who sought out his trusty subaltern, CDR O'Neill. And so it came to pass that my father ended up on Ike's staff at SHAPE - the planning center for the invasion of France and the final creation of the Western Front.

9

MY FATHER REMEMBERED

I was on the bridge of the high endurance cutter (WHEC) Spencer when a radioman handed me a message and said, "I'm sorry, Sir." The message read, "The U.S. Navy regrets to inform you that your father, CDR Robert E. O'Neill, USNR (ret.), died in Georgetown Hospital yesterday of a heart attack. Your mother and family are grieving and send their regards. Our condolences. J. A. McCain, ADM, USN, CINCPAC"

Was I Running from my father's absence?

Dad and I were close as I grew up. He was there for me (and my siblings as well), but as his only son, we seemed very close. From when I could first remember him holding me, praising me, instructing me in his firm, but not strict, manner to when we played golf or went sailing in the days before I left for Viet Nam, we had been friends and he was MY FATHER! I still cannot imagine a world without him and it was then already more than a year since he died.

Despite my persistent sadness, I decided to work on not spending my time being maudlin or indulging this recurring depression. Instead, I resolved to spend my driving time (besides not getting lost) on the positives of our relationship. That premise quickly led me back to sailing. This was the one sport that the two of us shared exclusively almost all of my life. At least once a year, no matter how busy our schedules, Dad and I coordinated our schedules so we could spend a day taking The Kate out onto Chesapeake Bay.

This musing brought back all the sailing lessons and how I came to learn about deep water, control a ship without an engine (we had one on the Kate, but rarely used it), and all of the nuances of interaction between the ship, the water, the tides and currents, the weather, and all of the traffic obstacles on the Bay (e.g., anywhere from crab pots to buoys to bridge supports). One drill taught me the whole point of ship mastery: the man overboard drill. At first, we practiced with a life preserver as the target. Dad was very good, but it took me awhile. Then one day, as we were just sailing, standing on the lee side with my face to the wind, I felt a hand press against my back and I was in space over the water, hearing a sound, "MAN..." Then I was in the water: surprised, fully clothed, and a bit panicked!

Surfacing quickly, I saw the Kate, my father at the helm beginning a maneuver that had me plucked from the water in a matter of 2 or 3 minutes. Strangely, the sight of the Kate and Dad had overcome my fear almost instantly. I realized within moments while treading water that my father was giving me a critical lesson in seamanship - all those lessons and drills had real-life meaning. He pulled me out of the Bay. Handed me a stack of towels and in no time, we were amiably discussing what had transpired and why it was done. I was either 12 or 13 at the time.

About 4 years later, the whole family had assembled for a 2 day sail from Chesapeake City up the Bay to Betterton-a pleasant 1/2 day sail. As we approached Betterton with little or no traffic on the bay and me at the helm, I heard a shout and a loud splash behind me. Dad had gone overboard. I called, "Man overboard!" The ladies were not emotionally ready for what followed. Dad was clearly visible. I threw the helm to full starboard. The Kate came about. I asked for and got a tack. Within a minute, two at the most, we were alongside Dad and assisting him into the Kate.

Much of the rest of the sailing day was taken up with the various ladies, including Kate herself at the helm and crewing. Except that about every 5 minutes, or maybe it just seemed that often, Dad would praise my sailing skills and talk about me becoming a man. I was about 15.

(As Catholics, we have First Communion and confirmation, about ages 8 and 12, marking movement to various stages of conscience raising and ethical responsibility. But the Jews with the Bar Mitzvah seem to have found the best right of passage to manhood [or Bas Mitzvah/womanhood].) From that day forward, I was schooled in advanced sailing techniques, navigation and Rules of the Road. My father was a patient, wise instructor who never seemed to be teaching-just communicating.

I reflected on my Dad's techniques for approaching and simplifying complex concepts must have played a key role in his becoming so successful in the insurance brokerage world in a relatively short time. I was hoping that I would develop some skills like his as I matured. In the course of the drive, I took inventory and decided that I did have skills that would help me succeed in the civilian world. I just hoped they would help me as a lawyer.

10

MOLLIE

(Two recordings: Not heavily edited. Some comments added.)

Chad Phelan was a basketball teammate and also a sophomore. He rarely played at 6′4″ and was not a great shooter or leaper. I was 6′5″ and had a good jumper and some very real lift. Also, I could play defense and was a willing passer: other than the point guards, one of a very few. So, I got minutes. Our freshman team was good, so my career was uncertain for the next 2 years. Chad's was in jeopardy.

Chad had a sister, Mollie, who was a first year at Immaculata, a Catholic women's college on the Philadelphia Main Line, not far from Villanova and Bryn Mawr, although vastly different. (Bryn Mawr was, and is, one of the "Seven Sisters" loosely aligned with the Ivy League schools, which were divided by gender based student bodies at that time. Bryn Mawr also had contributed Kathryn Hepburn. Villanova was a world class men's party school that played sports.)

On her first visit to her brother at Georgetown, Mollie and I hit it off quickly. We were both tall, and I suppose by the standards of the day good looking. Mollie was very verbal. My sisters were not shy when it came to speaking their minds, but Mollie put them to shame over a short time. Besides being good looking and almost 6 feet tall, Mollie did know her way around young men enough to get them talking and making them feel comfortable. That first weekend in D.C. in early December, we were never alone, but I had the sense we were together.

Georgetown was scheduled to play later that month in a holiday tournament at the Palestra (University of Pennsylvania

Fieldhouse —- old and legendary even by the mid 60's). Penn and St. Joe's, both Philadelphia colleges were also in the tournament. Our first game was at 1:00 on a Wednesday afternoon against an eastern team from upstate PA, Muhlenberg College. We trained up from D.C. and walked directly to the Palestra which was about¼ mile from the train station. We changed into our uniforms and were on the court by 11:30. I thought only about the game until it was over and we won. I played pretty well—about 16 minutes, 6 or 8 points with a handful of rebounds and a couple of assists. The next game would be the quarter finals on Thursday night at 6:30. Coach called a meeting for 10:00 next day and curfew for 11:30 that night. We bused to the Penn Center Inn hotel, a longish walk to the Palestra at 20th and Market Streets. I sat next to Chad Phelan during the short trip. I asked how I could get ahold of Mollie to see if she was free for the night. He responded something like, "That won't be a problem. She was at the game. She wants to see you and was hoping you would ask. She'll pick us up at 3:30. We'll go up to our house in Mount Airy and take it from there."

Mollie was on time. The three of us managed to cram ourselves into her VW Bug and took off up the East River Drive to the Wissahickon Parkway which leads up to Mt. Airy and the Phelan home. The Phelan's were great hosts and had been at that day's game as well. Mrs. Phelan was not only delighted to have Chad home, but seemed especially welcoming to me. Her son must have told her that my grandparents were from Germantown and Chestnut Hill. This seemed to make her very comfortable with the fact that I was not really from out of town. (Note: I have not mentioned an observable fact: a vast amount of Philadelphia natives, left to their own devices, rarely venture more than 100 miles from Philly - only locals can use the phrase "Philly." More on that point later.) We had very civilized cocktails. Mollie's younger brother, a high school senior, was invited to join the festivities. He was a player at Bishop McDevitt. The roaring fire, drinks and a roast beef dinner made for a pleasant evening. Mollie and I spent some time together, but not enough to really even talk among ourselves.

Around 8:30, Mr. Phelan said he had some things to discuss with Chad. He asked Mollie to drive me back to the hotel, indicating he would bring Chad in due course. With that, Mollie was up and, in moments, ready to go. After pleasant adieus and expressions of gratitude, we were in Mollie's VW heading back to Center City. She drove more slowly and we had a chance to talk. I asked her how she liked Immaculata. That was the right question for her. She had been to visit Chad on her own twice (meeting me on the second trip). She felt that being in Philly in a Catholic college was very much a continuation of high school. She wanted something different. Her grades were good but not great. Same for her college boards. She was seriously considering a transfer to American University or George Washington. She had been to Admissions at both and each seemed ready to admit her. What did I think? WOW!!

In response, I was forced to admit that, D.C. high school experience included, I was an ongoing product of the continuing Catholic education. There were differences—-DeMatha coming readily to mind (where I had played for legendary coach, Morgan Wooten, who would engineer the only upset victory of Lew Alcindor and Power Memorial of N.Y.C. during his 3 year tour [later becoming Kareem Abdul Jabbar].) Her enthusiasm was so evident, however, that I felt a need to give some level of credence to her concerns. That said: I knew so little about the curricula at both of her choices that I felt inadequate to discuss that topic. GW was a true city school with no particularly discernible campus. AU had a campus, an indifferent athletic program, but I knew little else about it. So, I gave a general response to her ideas.

Much to my surprise this brought a level of enthusiastic feedback which made Mollie appear almost joyous. I was uncertain about her apparent happiness as we arrived at the Penn Center Inn. I asked if she wanted to park and come in for a soda. After all, it was barely past 9; and, some of the other players, should they be around, knew Mollie was Chad's sister. She said she would look for parking and pulled halfway down the block away from the hotel entrance. Once there, she turned the car off and quickly leaned over to give me a delightful kiss. Later, when I walked her back to her car, the kiss was repeated with a serious hug. This scenario, with very slight variations, was repeated over the rest of the team's stay (we lost to St. Joe's in the final).

I thought good thoughts about Mollie, and saw her again in the Spring. She was transferring to American University in the Fall. Not totally certain why: I was pleased, but not overly excited.

Over the next 2 years, we were close, but not necessarily exclusive. The kisses became longer and more passionate at times. Our schools were less than 3 miles apart, but we rarely saw each other during the week. Studies at Georgetown did take up time. Mollie rarely talked about her classes. During the basketball season, I was very busy with my schoolwork, practice, travel and games. We did make time for each other; but too often, it felt like we were working too hard at our relationship. I started a few games and my playing time was increasing. The Hoyas had an exceptional record. We were getting notoriety—my name was mentioned from time to time. After we lost in the NCAA Eastern Regional, I invited Mollie on a family sail on the Bay before final exams started. (My family had met her on multiple occasions after games. Kate even suggested I invite her.)

Looking back, that day sail was the beginning of the high point period of our college relationship. We spent times that Summer entwining ourselves, but never getting very far. Mollie had begun to talk openly about a lifelong relationship. I was less certain. I really liked her, enjoyed our time together. Still, I was waiting to feel something, but I wasn't sure what. One night on the beach, Mollie took off her bathing suit top and I kissed her breasts. The experience was exciting and it was somewhat erotic; but with my sisters, I had seen enough of breasts that I was not overly aroused. Again, I was somehow a bit concerned about my inability to find something "Really Special" in our relationship (Looking back, I can see that I must have had a fear of commitment. My father and mother were so idyllic that I did not see Mollie and I at that level, perhaps not even close to it. Another factor was my own inexperience. In retrospect: I was not really "ready" for that level of commitment as yet.)

That Fall, early in my senior year, Mollie asked what I planned to do after college. (Secretly, I was hoping to keep playing basketball - for money.) I told her that I was not certain. She asked about grad school and I said I had not thought about it. Then she asked about Viet Nam. At that moment, I knew where she was going. Married men were supposedly going to be exempt from the draft. I had come to realize that I really liked Mollie, but I simply did not feel enough in love with her to consider marriage: that "spark" for which I kept looking just was not there. Still, we went on.

After graduation, I hooked up with a job at an energy company that had a very visible semi-pro basketball team. I got playing time in the same vein as at Georgetown - swingman-not quite tall enough to be a forward against very good big forwards, not quite quick enough to go up against very good guards. I began to see the handwriting on the wall. Then, one night, Dad called. He told me that Kate and Mollie had run into each other. Both of them were terribly concerned that I would be drafted. Thus, his call. He had asked around town and found out that the Navy Officer Candidate Schools were booked full for a year and they could not swear in reserves beyond that time without going on active duty as an enlisted. Undeterred, he had friends who were in the Coast Guard. He had an appointment for me in 3 days at USCG HQ in D.C. Would I come? The more we talked, the more sense it made. I went into the team leader's office the next morning and explained things. He was quite pleasant and said he understood full well. Turned out, I was not the first to come to a similar decision. I had dinner that night with my family and Mollie. When I had called to invite her, she said Kate had already done so.

After dinner, the two of us went for a walk. We talked seriously. We were suddenly grown- ups and there was a war raging 7,000 miles away. She wanted me to be safe, then she finally said it, "I love you. I don't want anything to happen to you." We kissed. I did not give the hoped for response in reciprocation.

The next day, I interviewed and was tested. All went well. The very next day I got a phone call asking me when I could report to OCS. My response must have been what the officer on the other end of the line wanted to hear. He told me to come in next Monday to be sworn in and to get my orders. He said they would notify my draft board. My family and Mollie seemed to breath a huge sigh of relief. My orders told me I would report on 1966 SEP 18 NLT 1500 to USCG TRACEN YORKTOWN, VA. I had 5+ months, a bit of money, a room at my parents' house and a girlfriend who would graduate in early June.

Kate had a talk with me about life, women, love, Mollie and the rest of my life. Dad had a talk or two as well. I was candid with them: telling them that I really liked Mollie but I was not sure she was "the one." It helped that I explained that I had seen them live their life and observed their love for my entire life. I saw and felt how they treated each other and the ways in which they meshed at times into an almost single being.

All that said, I still got the feeling that they both felt that Mollie was the one for me. We discussed options about how to deal with Mollie's graduation (no ring, if she expected one) and what to do to further advance and to test our relationship —- after all we had a good 3 months following her graduation. I saw Mollie quite a few times and things were at times uncomfortable. The word "love" no longer surfaced. I asked her what she was going to do after graduation. She said she was going to take the summer off and get a job in the fall.

Kate came up with "the solution." She and Mollie's Mom, both hoping for the same outcome, had put together a list of out of the area relatives for Mollie and me to visit over a 3 - 4-week span - a fully supervised courtship, if you will. Dad and Kate said they would pick up the expenses as part of "my going away to the Coast Guard present." The night before her graduation, I asked Mollie about the idea of the trip. Much to my surprise, Mollie seemed surprised by the suggestion. At first blush, she was almost put off, but when I laid out the involvement of our two mothers and the tentative itinerary, I could sense that she was warming to the idea quickly. At the end of that evening, she said words I will never forget, "Ronan, this trip, it's our last chance? Isn't it? I know I've told you I love you over the years any number of times, and I always hoped *I'd hear them back. I have just about given up. And, no, I did not expect a ring for graduation. But this, this may just work. I don't know. But since you are willing, so I must go. I have to know!"*

I still think about that summer with Mollie. Then, there was OCS. Back to USCG HQ. And Finally to Viet Nam. Nam was a last straw. (End of Session.)

11

OUR BEST SHOT:
MY MONTH WITH MOLLIE

(From a series of tapes and Dr. Arnaud's notes.)

Our mothers put their heads together, burnt up the telephone lines, and came up with about 15 options for Mollie and me to visit for our "supervised courtship," at least as they envisioned it. They presented us with a typed list. Mollie and I consulted at length. First, we each made a list of the places we each really wanted to go and we talked about some of them, particularly Cape Cod. We each then got to eliminate one form the other's list. I eliminated Niagara Falls.

Mollie struck none of mine. Then we saw how they would fit together as an itinerary. It was too long. After some study, I suggested we eliminate New York City and its 2 visits. We had a trip, gave the itinerary to the mothers, and they finalized the dates. In some cases, I would stay in a hotel, never Mollie - even with my relatives.

My parents had bought me a BMW 2002 sedan for my 21st birthday (Much like the Porsche Speedster or the VW Beetle, the 2002 was the model that began the mystique for the Bavarian Motor Works). Mollie still had her VW Bug. When I agreed that Mollie could drive sometimes, she agreed on my car. (I worried a bit the whole trip about something mechanical- no problems.) By 6:00 a.m. on a bright June morning, we set out on the burgeoning superhighway system called the Interstate.

Driving mostly through western Virginia, we arrived in Asheville, NC, at Kate's cousin Rose Ellen's house on the outskirts of this western North Carolina mountain city. Rose Ellen was beside herself with joy to receive visitors who were not her own children. Widowed during Korea with 3 children, she had married one of her first husband's platoon mates, a WWII veteran quite a few years older than her. When he retired after 22 years, they located back to his home town of Asheville. He had died last year, leaving her twice widowed!

After seeing our rooms and the house with its lovely gardens, we sat on Rose Ellen's back terrace and sipped home made lemonade. We talked about family for Mollie's benefit and then our plans for visiting the Biltmore Estate and driving the southern part of the Skyline Drive (the Blue Ridge Parkway in those parts) as well as going to Rose Ellen's favorite restaurant, my treat, tomorrow night.

After a Southern dinner of fried chicken, mashed potatoes and 2 green vegetables, Rose Ellen excused herself, leaving Mollie and me on her couch in the sitting room. Hearing her shut her bedroom door at the top of the steps, I moved closed to Mollie, put my arm around her, and after turning her a bit to face me proceeded to kiss her. When she began to respond, I backed away saying that we needed to be discrete, after all, this was the first night and if we were perceived as doing something untoward it would get back to our parents. Mollie pushed back further and I will never forget her words, "Ronan! We are not in high school. These are all adults and they expect a level of something from us. After all, this trip is set up for innocent promiscuity, not any type of passionate affair. Knowing you, that seems most unlikely!!"

***

Our time in Asheville was educational and filled with wondrous views, sites, sounds, good food and just enough of Aunt Rose Ellen who was a marvelous hostess. When we bid Rose Ellen adieu, we headed north on the Skyline Drive and into Virginia. About 30 miles past the Roanoke exit, we exited eastbound and headed to Lynchburg, a very hilly city in central Virginia. We stayed with Kate's cousin, Phillip and his wife, Krista. They had 3 children, one still at home. So, first I checked into a hotel and stowed my things while Mollie sat on the bed, eyeing me on occasion as I unpacked a few hang-ups. When I asked if she was ready, Mollie said, "This is the one flaw in their plan." And, she got up and we left.

By then I had the distinct impression, as I had on a few prior occasions, that Mollie would be a willing bed partner. I really did like her, but somehow, I was just not ready to make that leap. The Garrity's were wonderful hosts. Krista showed us around Lynchburg the next day as we took trolleys and repeatedly heard that this big town/little city was the San Francisco of Virginia. The trollies were fun! The evenings were pleasant, but the side trip to Appomattox was inspirational. We stood in the spots where Grant and Lee had stood on that fateful day that ended the fighting and started the Cold War between the North and South that was ongoing that day, and for years to come, arguably even now.

***

Then off to Baltimore to stay with one of Kate's WWII friends, Mary Anne Clarke, who had a small place, and so a hotel for me again. This time the room had a chair and Mollie sat in it while I quickly unpacked. No remarks before we departed to meet Mary and her surprise guest, Kate, for dinner. We had steamed crab, corn on the cob, beer, dessert, and spent quite a while talking. I dropped Mollie at Mary's place, and promised to return for breakfast. My mother rode back to the hotel with me. On the way, she wanted to know how "things were going with Mollie so far?"

My response did not cause her any cheer as I repeated some of the phrases I had used in the past, all coming down to not feeling that I loved her at the needed level to contemplate marriage, but not using those exact words about Mollie. We stayed at the same hotel, but Kate left early and I went to Mary's for breakfast with Mary and Mollie. We spent the best part of the day finding our way to Fort McHenry. Once there, we stood on its battlements looking down into the harbor where the British fleet had launched its barrage more than 150 years ago as a young American aboard one of its broadsiding battlecruisers began to write the words that would become the Star Spangled Banner.

The next day we drove west to Harper's Ferry through squalor and poverty rarely seen by but a few in our country: filth, unkempt properties, exterior electricity, appliances outside, abandoned cars and trucks - mostly cannibalized, naked children and people looking tired and woebegone! We visited the site of the arsenal where John Brown's Raid took place in what was, and still remained, an impoverished corner of the poor people of the south. That day, in its own way, stood in juxtaposition to our day at Appomattox but a few days before: so many lives lost, yet so many ideals unchanged despite the great generational sacrifice!

***

Now, we pushed on to Cape Cod, Mollie driving my 4-speed like a pro as we approached the home of Mollie's uncle, Ed, and his wife Helen on the outskirts of Yarmouth. Theirs was a 2 story house. Their bedroom was upstairs and they put us downstairs, but with the kitchen in between. This was to be our longest stay: 5 nights with day trips by ferry to both Nantucket and Martha's Vineyard.

Uncle Ed and Aunt Helen took us out to dinner that first night for, what else, Maine lobster. They had pre- ordered 4 lobsters and New England clam chowder (the white creamy one) as an appetizer, with a salad in between "to clear the palette." Mollie looked askance when she heard the menu and that it had been pre- ordered. I felt her tense and tried to read her expression, saying, "Mollie, Is something wrong?"

Her reply was a surprise of sorts, "My parents, despite all their time at the Jersey Shore, do not like shellfish, so I've never had most of the meal. But I don't want to be a killjoy!" Her expression betrayed her words, as did her loss of color.

As I tried to fashion a persuasive response, Uncle Ed stepped up with a solution, "Mollie, why don't you try each dish? And if you don't like it, we'll get you a quick replacement dish. This is a very obliging high-end restaurant that we frequent as regular resident customers."

Mollie had no sooner finished the last sip of her vodka martini, then her large cup of clam chowder arrived. Uncle Ed had the wine steward pour glasses of a French Burgundy Mollie stalled by taking a sip of the wine, then praising it effusively (good show by a 21 year old!). Finally, she consulted her soup spoon, skimmed some chowder from the top of the bowl, paused as it cooled and tried it. No visible reaction. She repeated the process twice more. Her stress seemed reduced. Then, Uncle Ed brought some reality to the situation, "Mollie, clams and most of the goodies in the chowder are on the bottom of your bowl. To appreciate how to proceed, please watch Helen."

Aunt Helen took her spoon, held her soup bowl at a bit of an angle, ran the spoon down the front of her bowl and across the bottom, bringing it to the surface on the far side of the bowl heaping with substances known to 3 of us, but not Mollie - whose eyes widened visibly.

Mollie swallowed. I thought I could hear it. She took her spoon and held it to mimic Helen's demonstrated angle, then followed Helen's course through her own bowl and brought it to the surface. With an "Here goes (audible gulp)," she put it in her mouth and chewed for the first time. As Mollie swallowed, a smile began to appear on her face.

The rest of the meal went seamlessly, except that the wine consumption was quite a bit more than what Mollie and I usually enjoyed (must have been its quality as well as the food it accompanied). The drive home was not that far (mercifully). Mollie's uncle and aunt by marriage asked if we would like a nightcap. We declined. They said "Good Night" and went upstairs to bed. At that moment, I thought maybe Mollie was right, we were not in high school, and we were being given a real chance to mate! But what to do?

Mollie was a step ahead. She turned out the hallway light at the bottom of the stairs. She took my hand and pulled me past my bedroom and the kitchen to her room, farthest from the stairs to our hosts' bedroom. In a low tone, she said, "They are so sweet. Kiss me!"

So, I did. Having drank a bit too much, I was concerned, but not as cautious as I should be. I pulled her close. Our kisses became passionate. She began to grind against me. I wanted to feel her skin. I peeled off her light sweater and could see the tops of her breasts. When we stopped for a breath, I began to kiss them. (We had gotten this far once before, but we were sober then!) Mollie made small sounds in her throat. They seemed to urge me on. Then, she seemed to pause for just a second or two. Something like an alarm went off in my head and I drew back. Mollie whispered, "Too much. Too fast. Too much to drink. (A pause.) One more kiss and off to your room. (Another pause.) If we were more sober, I might not have stopped." I left with those words.

That night helped shape my view of Mollie for years to come. First, she was more of a risk taker than I would have thought based on the "shellfish incident." Second, she was still willing to initiate our relationship despite my years of ineptitude. Third, she was no fool: no unprotected sex in a semi-drunken state. Mollie was more admirable than I thought.

***

The days and nights of Cape Cod were the high point of our time together. The days on the islands were almost poetic in their sights, sounds and smells, the bucolic weather, the rolling seas, the cool winds, even the way we held onto each other; and the way we clung to each other each night after my uncle and aunt went to their room.

With great reluctance, we bid a fond farewell to Mollie's uncle and aunt. We went around New York City using the Tappan Zee Bridge. We were spending two nights with Mollie's Aunt Phyllis, a single lady. She had a smallish home in Rumson, a very high-end NYC suburb. I was to spend the 2 nights at the Mollie Picher Inn in Red Bank, a few miles inland from Rumson and an antique capitol of the Mid-East coastline.

Mollie and I were in high spirits as we easily located her namesake hotel in Red Bank. We stopped there so I could check in before taking her to Aunt Phyllis' place in Rumson which was further from the Garden State tollway. We had breezed past NYC and were early. At the front desk, I asked if they had a pool. Of course, they did. She agreed. We went back to my car, parked, and while I brought my 2 bags, Mollie took out her swim things from a tote and we set off to my room.

While I put my hang-ups in the closet. Mollie went in the bathroom and returned wearing a fairly skimpy (by 1960's standards) bikini. I took a quick peak and said, "WOW!" Her blush ran all the way to the top of her breasts. I grabbed my swim things and changed quickly. On the way to the hotel pool, we went past the front desk and I explained we were going for a swim, and that Mollie was staying with her aunt in Rumson. We laughed and splashed and acted like a couple of kids 10 years younger. An hour flew bye and we toweled off, then returned to my room.

I asked Mollie if she wanted to shower first. She nodded yes and began to strip off her top right there. My jaw dropped. She said, "Would you like to touch them?" So, I did. And, we kissed. Next thing I knew we were on my bed with me kissing Mollie's breasts. I looked up and her head was back a bit, her mouth open. I paused. I thought. I stopped. Rolling next to her, I said, "Too much! Too much!! We cannot lose control like that. Something we could really regret might happen."

Mollie sat up very straight, swiveled, grabbed her top and was into the bathroom in a flash. She said not a word, but the look she gave me told me her emotions! She was not happy!! She said almost nothing until we were on the road to Rumson. Then, "You probably feel that I was trying to trap you into having coitus with me. No, Do Not Say Anything for a minute.

We had such a great day and a great time at the Cape, and we have been so careful. Then in a moment of spontaneity, you just stopped. Are you so afraid of letting go that you can't let us enjoy each other? No one needs to go all the way. There, I have said my part!"

Rather than speak without thought, I took a moment or two, "You are right. I'm sorry. You must think me quite an oaf, if not an unromantic prig. I do have feelings for you. I am a bit afraid of the sexual component of our relationship running ahead of the emotional part. I do not want to hurt you in any way, Mollie."

We had dinner at the Rumson Country Club and a nice visit with her aunt. I dropped them both at Phyllis' house, claimed that I was tired, and drove straight back to the hotel. I thought about Mollie all the way. I thought about us as I went to sleep. The next morning, I called her.

Asked her to tell her aunt we had to leave a day early. She agreed. I picked her up and we came back to the Mollie Picher. We swam and had lunch. We went back to our room. We made love, but stopped short of my climax. When we finished, smiling

Mollie leaned over me and said, "Was that so bad?"

We tried variations twice more before we set out for Long-port, NJ, our last stop at Kate's family's house with her sister present.

***

We proceeded to Kate's family home in Longport, NJ, occu-pied by her sister for purposes of our visit. It was a beach house of real consequence situated on a bit of a 10-15 foot bluff above the beach at high tide and built with an above-ground basement in the event of hurricanes and northeasters. Kate and my Dad were much more Chesapeake Bay people who loved sailing and the sea fare of the Bay to that of the ocean. This was only my third time to this family home.

Mollie and I were separated by floors with Mary Rose en-sconced between us. We had a good time, but those 5 days be-came a cooling off period of sorts in our relationship.

When I brought Mollie to her house in Mount Airy, we parked in front. Before she could say anything, I said, "What a marvelous time! I shall treasure it for the rest of my life. I wish I could say all the words you want me to say, but I simply can-not."

Mollie, turning to me with moist eyes, leaned over and kissed my cheek, "Only a few days now and you leave for Coast Guard OCS. I think we should call this our last moments together. Know, Ronan, that I love you. Know that I'll always love you. Stay out of harm's way. God bless you. See you around." And she was gone, just like that.

12

TINKER and THE USCG

(Another Session Tape/Notes)

USCG OCS is a bit like basic training crossed with some serious school- work. It's not to be confused with college and it is not an athletic camp. The drill instructors, one per platoon are not your friends. Your platoon mates may not be your friends. But if your roommate is your enemy, then you are in for a tough 20 weeks! My roommate was Seth Stevens and he was not my friend. Stevens was a first class radioman (RMl). Since he was an enlisted man, he would be a "mustang" if he was commissioned as an officer. Our platoon commander, P.G. Samuel was a mustang from Louisiana (that's LOO-See-Anna, if you are from there). They appeared not to care for one another on sight: a circumstance with collateral results for me as Stevens' roommate.

Joel Tinker bunked down the hall a few doors. We met first day. He was from the South Jersey Seashore, a town called Ventnor, went to St. Joseph's College in Philadelphia, a Jesuit school like Georgetown, but smaller and with far less name recognition. As the weeks in OCS played out, my time with Stevens came under strain again and again. A North Carolinian, he had little use for Yankees. Moreover, I had finished college (apparently he had not, although I was to learn later that his failure to do so was a direct result of what caused him so many issues, a failed accomplishment that seemed to cause Seth continuing heartburn)!

As a Yankee college grad with no prior USCG experience, I was of little value to Stevens. What it took me a few weeks to find out was that Stevens was not just any RM1, but he had been a "boot pusher" for enlistees at the USCG Training Center Cape May (as in New Jersey, as in the North!).That accounted for his patina of anger since he was being asked to accomplish a seemingly endless list of tasks, all of which he had mastered and most of which he was recently qualified to instruct or inflict, at his discretion. As a corollary to this, LT Samuels doubtless knew Stevens had been a drill instructor and was unwilling to allow this to do anything but hold Stevens to a standard higher than the mere OCS candidates. (As time went on, this was seen to repeat itself with more senior mustang candidates whom the OCS instructors saw as threats to their credibility {So, this subsurface tension seemed to be brought about not out of an authority issue, but perceptions of who knew what and relative self-worth . Turns out the USCG is not really that big.}.)

We had a platoon mate named Eli Einstein from Brooklyn. Nice guy who went to NYU -—- a Yankee, etc... Lt Samuel seemed to take an instant dislike to Einstein (appeared to be true of about half of us, but for most, it was temporary). On the first full day, we spent the a.m. getting our heads scalped, our uniforms issued, and receiving multiple briefings explaining how we were to use every minute of our days while in OCS — — scary at first blush. I watched Seth and began to observe what he treated as important. He figured that out quickly and began to hide some things from me. Finally, one night in our third week during study hour, I was trying to study and he was busy taking panels out of the ceiling. I asked him to stop making noise. He told me to "fuck off." I allowed that he did not have to be so rude. He called me a "prissy Yankee." I was up and he jumped off the chair on which he was standing and gave me a good shove. I shoved him back into his locker, knocking it a kilter and upsetting his carefully displayed uniform components as required in one of the early briefings. He seemed to grow bigger in his anger. (I was a good 4" and 40 lbs. bigger.) He pushed me aside and went for my locker, pulling it doors down onto the polished tile floor. Outraged, I brushed past him and grabbed his locker, swung around and was ready to throw it at him when two things happened: first, 3 or 4 other platoon mates burst into our room (presumably having heard the noise), and second, Seth began to laugh! He seemed truly pleased that I had stood up to him. He said little, but started by picking up my locker and putting it back. The others left. While we were policing the mess, we began to talk - as friends. He even learned that I was from south of the Mason-Dixon Line. (No matter: to him — D.C. and MD were Yankee outposts in the South.) Within a week, he was telling favorable stories about Cape May. (During inspections, all of our stuff that had no business being on display went in the ceiling. The SAT a.m. inspecting officers knew it had to be somewhere since neither of us had a car to put it in the trunk.)

At 9 weeks, Seth got a hand delivered letter. He was instantly overjoyed. He was selected for Chief Radioman (RMC). He explained that he got an unconditional 3 days leave with his promotion during which he had to get all of his uniform insignia redone and, most importantly, had to re-enlist right away to get a $15,000 re-enlistment bonus. He put on his RM1 uniform and headed to the Officer of the Day (OOD's) office. I didn't see him for 3 days. When he returned, he handed me a box and told me to put my stuff in it on Friday night and he would put it in his car. He lifted the blinds and pointed to the parking lot which you could see from one of our windows. I looked. The only thing new was a bright cherry red Corvette. I said, "No-o- o?!" Seth nodded his head!

***

While Seth was my roommate, Tinker became my best friend at OCS. We hung out together. We did calisthenics together. We rowed together. We had shared values and a lot in common.

During gym, we played basketball as did quite a few of the platoon members (Bravo-1). We were good. In the OCS class tournament, we went undefeated. I was relatively tall, Tinker was fast and good shot. Seth was tough and had played in high school as had several others.

Swimming and weight-lifting took up time as we neared the physical testing that every OCS candidate had to pass before he could go on the OCS cruise. I was a really good swimmer. Not everyone was. Those in danger of failing were called "sharks" and had to spend extra time developing their skills. Once we passed the test, we were freed from the swimming and weight classes UNLESS you were a Shark instructor-Tinker and I got that job. We had 6 sharks in the platoon (turns out that 3 of the 6 could not swim when they got to OCS), by the deadline test date we were down to 2 - one was Einstein. He was mine. Tinker had Dooling, another city guy.

Einstein could swim quite passably. He could dive in from the side of the pool. However, he was terrified of the tower jump and was having great difficulty learning to tread water.

Dooling had the same issues. For the final test, we were allowed to go up on the tower with them. Einstein drew the short straw and had to go first. He walked to the edge of the tower platform. Looked down 18 feet and froze on the spot. I told him, "Just step off and stay rigid." He said nothing and stood there. I peeked around his head and saw his eyes were closed. I said, "Eli, step forward on the count of 3 or else." I counted 3. Nothing. I pushed. Eli passed the tower jump. Dooling stepped off when it was his turn.

We had to get them to both tread water for 60 seconds but the examiner must have spent some time looking away as they got a bit of help and swam more than one or two strokes.

OCS was full of stories —- mostly positive, especially in retrospect. We had an OCS cruise, followed by Christmas leave, and a new platoon commander on our return for the final 3 weeks and commissioning. But the last big deal of OCS was your assignment. Before the OCS cruise, we each turned in our "Wish List" - 3 stateside assignments and 3 non-stateside, which included a few billets in Viet Nam. (Since the risk of actual assignment to Nam was so low and the number of non-stateside billets so few, most of us opted to volunteer, but not Tinker.)

When we returned, orders were beginning to flow into the Admin office for RESTRACEN YORKTOWN. With 2 weeks to go, the first assignment lists were posted. Many were assigned to high endurance cutters, a few to medium endurance, and the rest to an array of support billets at the district and group levels. Nothing for me, or Tinker, or Seth. All of the 95' WPBs were solely the province of USCG Academy grads. The 82' WPBs were skippered by very senior enlisted men, usually an E-8 or 9 chief.

The second list went up right before our final exams. Seth went to a buoy tender in West Palm Beach where he became XO in less than 4 months. Nothing for Tinker or me. The final list went up at the beginning of our last week. 22 names: 6 assigned to cutters being dispatched to Viet Nam; the rest, including Tinker and me to USCG HQ. Mine read: Report to Commandant (OFU-3), USCG Headquarters, 1300 Pennsylvania Avenue, Washington, D.C. no later than 0800 on 1967 January 29. Details, many of them, followed. Tinker and I were both stationed in D.C.

One of the things you can come to love about the federal government is that it is a truly non-profit organization. Tinker was assigned to the Chief of Staff's offices. I was assigned to Floating Units, part of the Office of Operations. USCG HQ was located at 1300 Pennsylvania Avenue then as it was part of the Treasury Department (1500 Pennsylvania Avenue) and had been since its inception as the Revenue Cutter Service late in the 18th Century. Floating Units were usually cutters. This was considered a choice assignment. That was all about to change.

One of my first collateral assignments was to be OFU's Classified Material Control Officer- a potentially daunting task. At the start of my second week came the advice that 26 cutters of the 82' patrol boat class (WPB, with all USCG designations starting with 'W') were to be assigned to Viet Nam for patrol duty. The rationale was their ability to go where the US Navy vessels could not. I was part of the staff tasked with selecting, organizing and arranging to get these cutters to Subic Bay in the Philippines where they would be refitted for that duty and be given their final deployment orders.

Tinker was assigned by the CCS to act as junior liaison for personnel transfers between the Personnel staff which cut orders and OFU which was providing the vessels. Not all crew was retained. 2 junior officers were assigned to each 82' WPB, which normally had a MCQM or MCBM as the Officer-in Charge. This billeting shift represented a far more complex process than it would appear superficially. Moreover, in order to interact with the USN, a fair amount of personnel shuffling as well as modifications to the cutters were needed. All of this was to take time which was not perfect as a war was being waged in Viet Nam.

Then, in the midst of all of this activity came a notice from the Commandant that the entire Coast Guard was to be reorganized along "mission lines" as opposed to its current organization along "asset type lines." That change was to be affected on 1 APR 1968, presumably immediately after the 82' WPBs sailed for Long Beach where they were to be transported by a much larger vessel to Subic Bay.

Interestingly, we worked a regular day at USCG HQ from 0730 to 1630 every day. No one appeared to work overtime. Getting typing done was extremely difficult, especially as your rank got lower (Ensign was realistically the lowest rank). Still, the work was getting done in a timely fashion. During down time, I organized and documented classified material, a great deal of which went back to WW II. (Some of which I persuaded the authorities could be destroyed —- generating even more paper work.) And, then there was the USCG HQ basketball team which played in the federal agency league on Monday— Thursday nights at 1900 or 2030 in the basement of the Interior Department, which had a full sized court. Upon arrival, Tinker and I were immediately contacted. That was on a Monday. On Wednesday night we were in uniform and saw playing time. The next week, we were both starting.

So it was that Tinker and I became closer friends. We began to discuss rooming together. I saw some of Mollie and we commuted north twice together on weekends. Then, 2 days before scheduled departure to begin the trek to the Philippines, we learned that the XO of the Point Arena had been severely injured in an initial outfitting accident in Long Beach. An immediate replacement was needed. OFU looked around and saw me. Personnel agreed.

I got orders that day to report to Long Beach not later than (NLT) 3 days hence, along with a plane ticket from Dulles Airport to LAX. The next day, my last at USCG HQ, Tinker came up to me and showed me his orders. I thought he was coming along! No!! He was replacing me. (MORE on that later.)

I called Mollie. She said, "Good-bye and good luck." That was all. Kate and Dad were in shock. They took me to dinner that last night-just the 3 of us. I will never forget that dinner OR my mother's tears-despite all of their efforts, her only son was going to war!

13

TO SAUSALITO

(A Recording)

When I heard from the various law schools, there were no real surprises. I did not get into any of the really, really good ones - Harvard or Stanford, but I did get into UC Hastings. I called Tinker to let him know. He seemed very pleased, especially when I told him I had signed up. When I asked him about finding a place, he told me a two bedroom at Cote d'Azur had just given notice, so if I would sign up for a year, we could room together. I agreed readily. We spoke almost daily for the next week.

Then, I began to get ready to leave. The initial packing was no big deal, but I could tell Kate was unhappy because she absented herself whenever I went to work on things.

Finally, I cornered her and we had another talk. She tried to put a happy face on things, but she clearly was not up for my leaving. In the end, I took almost no furniture as Tinker told me he had found some great deals from graduating third years. So, I fit everything into my '66 Mustang and a small U-Haul trailer. I planned to spend 10 days seeing America as I made my way to Sausalito.

It was an overcast, muggy morning when Kate and I said our final good-by. She had hosted a bar-b-que for family and a few friends the night before, but it ended early as I had to get up by 5:30 to get off with the beginning of the rush traffic. Once I made it across the 14th Street Bridge to 1-95, I would be home free as the commute into D.C. would be coming from the opposite direction in Virginia. By 7:00 a.m., I had settled down and hoped to make it to the Atlanta suburbs for the first night.

On that leg of the drive, I realized I would have more time to think than I had in years. Worse still, I quickly realized that in my haste to leave greater D.C. and start my new life, I was being less than honest with myself on a number of fronts.

***

When I got off the plane from Dulles at LAX, I was greeted by an azure blue sky, warm air and no humidity. An enlisted man was holding a placard with my name on it. After identifying myself s Ensign O'Neill, we claimed my duffel and suitcase from checked baggage, proceeded to a motor pool sedan, and my driver named in an anonymous sense, Smith, took me ever so slowly through bumper-to-bumper traffic down 1-495, the Long Beach Freeway {"World's Biggest Parking Lot" according to Smith), exiting at *the Port* of Long Beach. He pulled up to the Point Arena, took my 2 bags out of the trunk, shook my hand, wished me luck and was gone. All I could think, and I still remember, I never learned his first name.

Walking over to the 82' cutter, I looked around for an officer who would be the CO. I remembered he was a LTJG named Torrez. Could not recall his first name. An enlisted man in soiled fatigues came over to me and ID'd himself as Boatswain's Mate Second Class (BM2) Peterson. He told me that Mr. Torrez was over at the Squadron CO's Hut and suggested that that would be the best place for me to report. Then he volunteered to take my 2 bags and put them in my "cabin." Turning, he added, "You best consider sending some of your clothes home. Space on board is at a premium."

I headed in the direction that Peterson indicated and quickly came upon the Squadron CO's hut. The meeting room was crowded with junior officers, most of them in work fatigues. One was not: LTJG Torrez stood out. The ribbons on his chest shown like new and his name tag appeared polished it was so shiny. One look told me Torrez was a Mustang and my stomach went instantly uneasy. The SCO came over to greet me. LCDR Wilcoxon introduced me first to my CO, LTJG Torrez who stepped forward, offered his hand to shake, then added, "Welcome Aboard, Ensign O'Neill. I look forward to working with you." That said, he dropped his grip and turned his full attention back to the SCO's briefing.

The next morning LTJG Torrez had disappeared. I never learned what happened to him. His replacement, arriving the next day from San Francisco, was LTJG Tom Stone. In seemingly no time, the Point Arena was loaded aboard the transport with another 8 WPBs and we were bound for the Philippines.

14

TO SAUSALITO:
VIETNAM RECALLING THE BEGINNING

Despite my attempts to block those thoughts, I could not completely avoid ruminations of my time in Viet Nam. On the trip, I came to realize that leaving the Coast Guard was perhaps my real first step in putting those experiences behind me. Rather than present them as they randomly came up during my drive across country, in my dreams, and in my sessions, I try to present a brief, sometimes, terse chronology of my primary, recurring recollections.

Driving through the cotton fields of Louisiana, my mind drifted to the Trident's arrival at Subic Bay in the Philippines, the actual headquarters for Commander in Chief, Pacific ("CINCPAC"). The U.S. forces were nearing the peak of their build-up. The U.S. Navy's facilities were everywhere: huge floating dry docks, warehouses, cranes, and ships of every description, including a battleship, an aircraft carrier and scores of smaller warcraft and support ships.

The Seventh Fleet had functionally shifted its operational base from Pearl Harbor to this natural harbor on the west coast of that country's main island, Luzon. None of the vessels were anywhere nearly as small as the 82' WPBs on board the Trident. My unspoken feeling was that since our small cutters are not real warships, why are we here?

The man heading up the U.S. war effort was a 4 star admiral. He had served with distinction in my Dad's war. He was from a Navy family and he had sons in the Navy. He was ADM John McCain. His base was not in Viet Nam itself, but onboard an aircraft carrier. The U.S. Navy ("USN")'s air arm controlled the

skies of Viet Nam. The U.S. Air Force (USAF) delivered ordnance on demand in vast quantities and supplied some ground
support. The Marines and the Army each had an air arm as well,
but it was the USN which made the bulk of the tactical air
strikes. It was ADM McCain who decided what service, planes,
and targets were to proceed with every specific mission. Even
when it came to major tactical troop movements, it was this admiral, sometimes with input from a president, who had the final
command say on who went where to come to grips with the
enemy.

The war had become a political football: at home, protestors
marched and sometimes rioted - some draftees left for Canada
rather than serve. In the war theatre itself, the themes of Korea
were beginning to play out: do not bring the Peoples Republic
of China (PRC) or the Russians (USSR) directly into the war.
Also, there was the problem of Vietnam's neighbors in that their
sovereignty needed to be respected. Meanwhile, the Army of
North Viet Nam (ANVN) and its guerilla affiliates in the south
were unconstrained in their use of their neighbor's spaces to
move troops, supplies and weapons in both directions. It was
like going into a fight with one hand tied behind your back.

Although we did not know the precise details of where we
would be, we had a pretty good idea of what we would be
doing. No war had ever been reported by the news media like
this one. Everyone who cared to know could figure out about
what was going on with the Americans in Viet Nam. All you had
to do was watch your television. Of course, this same information was all equally available to the enemy.

So, we believed that we would be deployed to stifle arms and
war supplies movement south along the coast. The 82' WPBs
were relatively shallow draft and capable of very good maneu-
verability at very low speed. Thus, they could ply the coastal
waters with the hundreds of miles of inlets, rivers, creeks, villages - large and small -and thousands of small water craft

capable of smuggling armaments. Of course, those same small vessels could also smuggle the Viet Cong ("VC"), but they were always civilian in disguise, so these guerillas could move about essentially undetected. This was a blueprint of our evolved assessment on our voyage, but still contained a good deal of speculation.

Our superiors had been silent on the actual deployment and what it would mean. So it was that the day after we landed in Subic Bay, 52 junior officers assembled in a briefing room at the USN HQ.

CDR Pete Lund was the direct commander of RONONE as the 26 boat squadron was to be known. He stood on an elevated platform at a lectern. A number of Navy brass and a CG LCDR were also on the platform. Behind him was a chart showing the northern half of the coast of South Viet Nam. At the very top was North Viet Nam with a bold red line marking its border with the south. Alpha labels appeared in descending order on the chart; Northernmost was A-11 denoting villages "of consequence." These were large enough to have fleets of fishing boats, perhaps some junks, and to harbor their own guerillas (the VC).

Apparently the backing of the chart was magnetic. CDR Lund took a name plate saying Pt Leopard and placed it opposite A-10. He said the border south to, and including, A-9 was to be the Leopard's "usual area of patrol responsibility" - that coast include a number of deep inlet and small rivers. Leopard was responsible for all navigable water within 3 miles of the coast as well as the navigable inlets.

Next at A-6, the speaker put up a placard saying PT Arena. I felt myself reflexively inhale a deep breath. My palms suddenly felt wet. This was really it - war! At that moment everyone began to stand and come to attention. An entourage of khaki uniforms entered the room, one of them had shoulder boards with a wide gold bar and 3 smaller gold bars. ADM John McCain moved directly to center stage. He saluted the stage, then audience.

His first words were "As you were." Chairs shuffled and people returned to their seats. The Admiral turned to CDR Lund saying, "With your permission CDR, I would like to address this group of officers for a few minutes?" The CDR said, "At your pleasure, Admiral."

"Gentlemen, I appreciate your show of naval etiquette; however, moving forward, remember that this is a combat operation and formalities should be kept to an absolute minimum. If we meet in the future, a salute will suffice.

"By this time you have doubtless come to understand the basic mission you are here to undertake. You are in the process of becoming familiarized with the coast and waters of this country and with your areas of primary responsibility. Remember, we are a team.

You are all Coast Guard, but we are in a war zone. As you also know, in this zone, you are under the command of, and functionally a part of, the United States Navy. You are part of that bigger team. You will have your own team-RONONE. The Coast Guard is in the process of deploying 6 high endurance cutters to act as supply, back up and floating bases for you. That will be RONTHREE. 5 of them will be on duty at all times. They will be in place when your patrols begin in about 10 days.

"This mission may be more dangerous than it will seem most of the time. Your primary mission will be to identify the infiltration of weapons and ordnance into the south. We expect that you will be able to deal with small numbers of sampan and smaller junks.

However, this is where you need to exercise prudence. Not all junks are as they may appear. Some may be armored and some may have camouflaged firepower. Anything bigger than a junk - a trawler or ANVN patrol boat should not be engaged. These junks and trawlers are especially dangerous. Those of you patrolling near the border must be especially alert.

"If there is any question of unequal firepower, you are not, I repeat NOT, to engage, or even attempt to engage. I repeat: your primary mission is to identify. Your secondary mission, and of essentially equal importance, is to preserve the integrity of your craft and the safety of your men so you can continue to undertake your primary mission. Once you are satisfied that you have met the conditions I have discussed, you may intercept perceived enemy craft.

"What I will not do is discuss boarding of the watercraft you will routinely encounter. That is a Coast Guard specialty and that is why you are here. Finally, I am not instructing you to run from a fight if one should find you. If there is a fight, I will expect you to engage the enemy and defeat him. For the duration of this conflict, you are considered to be part of the Navy. I am thoroughly familiar with the Coast Guard's record when called upon in times of national conflict. If you men live up to that tradition, you will bring honor to yourselves, the Coast Guard and your fellow countrymen. I wish you every success in the discharge of your duty. God go with you.

With that remark, the Admiral shook CDR Lund's hand, waved at us and was gone trailing a khaki column of officers behind him.

15

TO SAUSALITO: THE BLOCKADE

After the initial briefings, we were returned to the cutters. We knew the WPBs were to be modified significantly at Subic Bay and that process was already underway. Machine gun mounts were being welded into place on the superstructure. A winch was removed from the foredeck and a mount of some type was being put in place. This turned out to be a device to accommodate an .81 mm. Mortar with a .50 cal. machine gun mounted on top. Another mount aft also held a .50 cal. while four .20 cal. were housed two on each side of the superstructure. Considering that these boats had no actual armament and were not built to be weapons platforms, this was useable fire power for a small fight if the other side did not have large caliber weapons or an overwhelming firepower advantage.

As was the case with all USCG patrol craft, the 82's were painted white, the calling card of the ever peaceful Coast Guard. But now, in a war zone, the WPBs were war vessels and were repainted with camouflage tans, black, greys and other murky colors. Some equipage below decks was redone, but the conversion went quickly and in less than 2 weeks virtually all of the cutters were ready to begin their patrols with the primary mission being the interdiction of weapons, munitions and supplies from north to south along this quirky, indented and difficult to navigate coastline with its small rivers, creeks and the overgrowth of the jungle like fauna: so many places to hide, so few eyes to ferret out the smugglers. Finally, recall that all of the locals looked alike. The Viet Cong did not wear uniforms, rather they fit right in with all the other inhabitants. The net result was we would not know the enemy when we met him. Our defense was vigilance and awareness. Our best weapons were our imagination, creativity, background intelligence from the Navy, and our ARVN liaison officer, LT Li.

Li was a pleasant appearing Catholic Vietnamese from the Saigon area. He was the product of a good family, received a commission in the Army of the Republic of Viet Nam (ARVN), and promptly applied to be part of its Navy. Because of his age and background, he was selected for a special course with stints at Annapolis and Yorktown, the Coast Guard Reserve Training Center for its reserve officer corps. Many of the courses included instruction in English which meant that by the time LT Li reported aboard the Point Arena, he was a highly competent communicator in English for a native Vietnamese.

The coast north of Cam Rahn Bay was divided into 9 segments to the border with the northern border at a blind point. Point Leopard was assigned A-9. Point Arena was reassigned A-8. Point Mendocino was A-7, and so on. Our support cutter was the 327' WHEC Taney, which cruised from 3 - 5 miles offshore. The winter monsoon was moderating and with its end, the arms smuggling season would begin. Point Arena was on station for Christmas 1968.

The first patrols were more about familiarization then attempts at intercepting arms smugglers. But as the weather began to moderate the number of sampans in the close-in coastal regions began to multiply exponentially. No two necessarily looked exactly alike, but the points of differentiation were so slight as to defy actual classification. The same was true of the occupants. All the Vietnamese sampan crews did not look exactly alike, it was just that there was so little difference between them. The issues were obvious almost from the outset: how were we supposed to investigate at least hundreds, if not thousands, of small water craft that all looked essentially the same?

In less than 2 weeks, we had an answer and were attempting

to implement a solution: put a hull number on every craft. It was not a question of a census. We knew the rough home area of each (at least LT Li claimed he got that data) and we affixed a number on the gunwale of each sampan. Before long, the majority of the vessels had numbers. We did boardings. We were pleasant. We searched under seats and in compartments, if there were any. In the end, after more than a month, we had found nothing!

There were also junks and trawlers. The junks were theoretically wooden, the trawlers steel and usually NVN even if posing as civilians. The junks could be motorized, armored, or both. These 2 classes were considered highly suspicious and were always subject to search. But it was the sampans, their sheer volume that lead LTJG Stone, our Commanding Officer (CO) and me (XO) to think that somehow these were the primary means of smuggling. So how was it done? We began to patrol at night without our lights.

First, we encountered a big sampan, low in the water. Its crew was obviously shocked when we appeared seemingly from nowhere. They did not resist and we had our first real arms and munitions cargo. This made us realize that the VC might be sending us what they wanted us to inspect, so we needed to become more creative. We came up with a means of passing a rope under the sampan being inspected (they had no keel or rudder) to encounter submerged packages attached to the hull. This yielded results. Fishing lines aplenty played out from each sampan. Following random lines to their ends proved fruitful. All manner of means was used to make lines appear to track fish, when in fact they trailed illicit cargo. In a matter of months, the blockade was getting smarter and the results more effective.

On a night patrol, a junk was silhouetted against the feint lights on the shore. Slowly, we approached. It was a moonless night. The junk must have caught sight of us. It began to run. It was motorized. The Point Arena sprang to full life, searchlights illuminating its quarry. The junk increased speed, but was losing separation. Its captain turned toward shore somehow sensing safety there. We closed. At about 200 yards, the junk opened automatic fire. GMl Rafftery opened up with the .50 cal. gun. The junk exploded in a shower of fireworks!

The next day, it was back to the continuing tedious searching and occasional numbering. War was also dull.

16

TO SAUSALITO: A-8

In addition to the section of coastline patrolled by Point Arena being denominated A-8, its largest village also had that same designation. (Every little place in South Viet Nam had its own name; however, most of them were not recorded anywhere and no one began to know all of them, or how to tell them apart.) A-8 had the biggest fishing fleet. It had some organization that made it look like a village, and it had quite a few people in addition to fishermen. (We assumed it had its own resident VCs.) A-8 sat on a peninsula.

The village appeared timeless. It was there when we came. It would be there when we left. The huts were thatched-bamboo and palm fronds - raised 2 or 3 feet off the ground to let the monsoon rains and floods flow underneath and hopefully to survive whatever tsunami might appear without warning. Every morning at least 10 or 15 sampans put out to fish. Some days that number was much greater. LT Li had no success gaining an understanding of the variables associated with the number of craft and fishermen. In all, these locals were a tight lipped group. The fish, together with the production of their meagre rice paddies, provided the bulk of sustenance for this village (and most others with which we became familiar). The poverty and squalor were not what we had expected to find. A-8 held no fascination for the men of Point Arena.

On a moonless January night, close and muggy, we made our way south and stood off about half a mile out from the beach at the point of A-8. The plan was to come in fast early the next morning with the rising sun at our backs and to inspect all of the fishing craft as they were beginning the process pf launching. LTJG Stone and I thought that increasing random appearances instead of a fixed patrol might facilitate more success. We were forced to conclude that our entire process was too predictable and the VC could feed us an endless supply of empty quarry.

SN Caselli was asleep on a mat on deck. A sea drogue was helping us maintain our position without engine noise. QMC Terwilliger was keeping watch on the beach and the peninsula. It was about 0345. Suddenly the blackness of night was broken by a flash of light and a muffled sound. We awoke instantly! Spilling onto the bridge, Chief Terwilliger reported a hut appeared to be in flames. Perhaps more than one hut. LTJG Stone and LT Li also came to the bridge. I suggested that we jettison the sea drogue and head into the beach. I mentioned a possible trap and all 4 of us concurred. As we moved in, we fashioned a plan.

The sounds were coming from the center of the village, not the beach. The hut that appeared afire seemed about there also. Sudden shrieks pierced the air. I could see no more than the chief described when we had come on deck. We considered options and asked Caselli to get the rest of the crew on deck. It might be just a bad fire. It might be VC. It could well be a trap. LT Li could offer nothing else.

The skipper and I conferred. We asked QMC Terwilliger to bring the crew together. GM1 Rafftery broke out weapons. We divided into groups: ENC Staller with ET2 Jones and Caselli stayed on board with the CO. The latter two each at a .20 cal. and the .50 cal. LT Li lead one group which was to circle left and approach the village obliquely. I had 2 men to approach frontally. The cutter and my landing boat would make a lot of noise. Li would approach surreptiously. As we departed, a call went out for Swift boat back-up.

Chief Terwilliger was with Li. Gunner Rafftery was with me. The Li's group on the rubber launch pushed off and began to

circle in. We rode in a distance until LTJG Stone brought Point
Arena to a standstill and we launched the skiff directly at the
beach. In the darkness, we could not make out anyone on the
beach. Beached boats were everywhere. There were no lights
and no gunfire. The fire was unabated. The screams seemed to
increase in pitch and intensity. In minutes we were on the beach.
We proceeded forward cautiously using the fishing craft as cover
as we began to approach the village itself which was set back
from the beach to allow it to deal with monsoon winds and tides
as well as the occasional tsunami. Suddenly, there were several
shots. The screaming almost completely stopped. We advanced
among the huts. Several of the men saw us and ran toward us.
They were unarmed. They signaled to come forward. I proceeded slowly and hoped my men would do the same.

The bulk of the villagers were pressed up against the trees
on the far side of the village which was shaped in a rough oval.
In the absence of the screams, there was sobbing, some sounds
like rumbles and an occasional shout. We looked around for anyone who appeared armed. We saw no one.

LI and his men were nowhere to be seen. Rafftery, Foreman
and I pressed forward into the open. No one fired. Still, we proceeded slowly. I watched ahead. They eyed our flanks. We
moved from hut to hut toward the open oval in the center of the
village. Terwilliger and Jacobsen appeared on the left. We moved
more deliberately. Most of the villagers shrank away. Where was
LT Li? He spoke Vietnamese. None of us did. Terwilliger said
that Li and he got separated in the dark. Foreman tried some
French on the first villagers we encountered. None of them responded verbally, but they did point toward the end of the oval
farthest from all of us.

I approached the crowd. A small woman blocked the way. I
touched her shoulder. She turned. Her vacuous eyes fell on my
M-16. Then she looked at my face and her eyes seemed to mist
up. She turned and pushed the woman in front of her and we

slowly made our way through the crowd. The villagers were short people. A girl approached. I asked Jacobsen to speak to her. He did. She responded in French. The VC had been there. Four of them. They accused an elder, Xan Hun Thuy, of failing to cooperate with them. They woke the village. The girl moved toward the open oval. The crowd parted. She said that the VC had taken Thuy's family from their hut. The oldest boy failed to cooperate and a blow from a machete opened his skull and he had dropped on the spot-right in front of us, we could see where he bled out.

The VC leader told the assembled village that they intended to make an example of Thuy and his family. The leader opened Thuy's stomach with what sounded like a parachute knife. The wife and other children watched. Foreman became visibly upset. They moved closer to where Foreman stood. The crowd moved away. Nothing prepared me for what I saw. There was a woman and her son lying in a pool of their conjoined blood both of their throats slit. A few paces away were 2 girls, teenagers if that old, naked below the waist, lying in a heap. Also part of that heap was a man with grey hair. Trailing from his stomach were his intestines. They ran to a tree a few yards away. The intestines wrapped around the tree. We could tell between what the girl said and what we saw that Thuy was tortured by running him around the tree, pulling his intestines from his abdomen, then, he had been made to kneel and watch his daughters raped, his wife and other son executed with that same knife, his raped daughters shot, and only then was he executed last, toppling on top of his daughters, perhaps in his final act of love.

The sight of these innocent deaths was excruciatingly gut wrenching. Yet the perpetrators might remain in the area. Lt Li was missing. The girl said little more. Then the Swift boats arrived. Marines were onboard. Two of them spoke Vietnamese. Little more detail was forthcoming. No one from the village went fishing that day. Two days later, we were advised that Lt

Li was found in a bunji trap. The poisoned spikes hidden beneath a false piece of earth had impaled him causing what was yet another agonizing death.

As XO and leader of the relief party, I had the duty to identify LT Li and report on his death. I also had the duty to report on the slaughter at the village which we called A-8.

That memory lingers. It surfaces in my dreams. It played out more than once as I drove toward Sausalito. I hoped it would fade. It was not something I shared with anyone. Perhaps I should have.

17

TO SAUSALITO: THE ROUND-UP

L T Son replaced Lt Li. He was quiet. He asked what happened to Li and he became even more quiet when told by me. This followed a week of Rand R. I chose Honolulu. Bad idea: spent my week drinking and trying to forget.

Back on station, The CO and XO of Point Leopard joined LTJG Stone and me on the WHEC Sherman. The Navy wanted to try something new: herd a large group of sampans together and inspect them, including using a few Navy Seals to check the keels for attached cargo or lines. Each of us got a guest Seal. Sounded like a reasonable plan.

It had no success. Did the VC have spies?

18

TO SAUSALITO—QUANG TRI

As the weather got cooler, the action in the interior of South Viet Nam began to increase. The U.S. Army and Marines were to go on offense to clean up VC and ANVN between the Delta and the northern border and to eliminate as many enemy troops as and arms caches possible. This had been going on for a few weeks as the New Year approached. Point Arena continued its patrols focusing between A-9 and A-12. (The numerical areas numbers were reassigned as experience taught where assets and potential threats were more prevalent. The areas just south of the border, starting now with A-12 were less populated and had fewer vessels than previously counted. The reasons were unclear, but fear of the VC may have had quite a bit to do with that.) With ongoing losses and break-downs, other 82' WPBs had been drawn away for other assignments. For the last 2 days, light artillery and small arms fire was audible, some of it not far inland. With the fighting near the coast, few fishermen were going out. They must be staying in their villages to prepare to move if the fighting came their way. Of course, some of them were doubtless VCs.

Off A-11, RM Ginger reported receiving a message from US NAVY COMMAND to the effect that a platoon of Marines was separated from its company and pinned down at the village identified as A-9. Pt. Arena was ordered to proceed to A-9 and participate in evacuating those Marines. QM Terwilliger handed the coordinates to LTJG Stone. A course change was quickly made and the cutter began to move at its flank speed of about 18 knots.

In 10 minutes we could hear the sound of weapons. In another five, we could see the Marines, through our binoculars, all in a smallish area in the middle of the village. They were using a couple of buildings nearest the water as cover and exchanging fire. A few Marines were down by the waterline.

Stone checked with Terwilliger and the tide would be running in for the next hour - not perfect as the cutter would be pushed toward the shore as it tried to board the troops. Slone conned the Pt Arena toward shore in a zig-zag pattern, but the enemy was concentrating its fire on the Marines. The heaviest fire was coming from a few buildings at the southern edge of the village or just inside the overgrowth nearby. Stone told me to take charge of fire suppression. I immediately ordered GM Rafftery to open fire with the 81 mm mortar, providing him with firing coordinates which changed as the cutter changed course and drew nearer to the shore.

At about 400 yards, we opened fire with the 2- .20 caliber guns. The mortar rounds appeared to be slowing the advance of the VC. Hard to tell with the machine guns. As we began to draw nearer to the beach the elevation of the mortar was getting so low that it could not be used. At about 200 yards, I ordered Rafftery to depress the mortar and open fire with the 50 Cal. mounted on the mortar. The opening rounds devastated a few of the VC. Then, they renewed their pressure with increased intensity. Most of the Marines were at the waterline and a few were in the water. Our fire was now the major suppression to cover them as they waded out toward us. At about 100 yards, Terwilliger told Stone that the bottom was coming up quickly. The CO ordered the engines on minimum to hold the cutter in place. The Marines were wading fairly rapidly, but half were still close to shore. The first of them were hoisted on board. They moved to the gunwhales to return fire to the beach and provide further cover.

Fire opened up from the north end of the village. I ordered

one of the 2 - 20 Cal. and the Marines to open suppressing fire there. Terwilliger told Stone that the tide was pushing the boat dangerously close to grounding. (If the propellers became stuck in the bottom, the Point Arena would be at the mercy of the tide and the VC.) So, as the last of the Marines began their wade out to the WPB, it began to slowly back away. But for the fact of being in a firefight, this might have appeared funny. Finally, Stone stopped. The last of the Marines began to clamber aboard and suddenly heavier automatic fire began to come from the beach. I moved to the ladder area, keeping low. The last Marine was almost in my grasp when he threw his head back. I reached out, grabbed his wrist and pulled. He came aboard literally on top of me. I yelled, "That's all of them!' Stone threw the engines in reverse for about 50 yards, then swung the cutter about and we headed away from the beach with what was left of a platoon of Marines on board. Some were bleeding badly, including the one on top of me.

Da Nang was the nearest base with medical facilities. We had Ginger radio USCG Support and US NAVY COMMAND. No floating help was in the area, so they told us to proceed due south. My Marine with the leg wound was given a tourniquet and the bullet hole which seemed to go completely through the flesh of his leg was plugged as best we could with bandaging.

He appeared to be the most seriously injured. The Marines hunkered down and were quiet. We sought no information and they provided little. It was clear that they had left teammates behind. They were morose!

Shortly before dawn the next day we were escorted to a wharf at Da Nang. The Marines began to disembark. Stretcher bearers took the man with the leg wound out of my bunk and put him in an ambulance. More than half the Marines had wounds, Miraculously, the Point Arena crew was unscathed. The last Marine off, a sergeant with 3 stripes addressed the CO and me, "We always called the Coasties 'Shallow water Sailors.'

It's a damn good thing you are, or none of us would be here. I guess I'm the senior survivor. I intend to let my CO know what you and your men did. May the wind stay at your back!" With that he went down the gangway.

Minutes later, we got orders to report back to our duty station.

19

TO SAUSALITO—TO DANANG

On the run to DaNang, I had no bunk, so I stayed on deck. After the first watch, I grabbed some coffee and hunkered down against a forward gunwhale to avoid the engine vibration as much as possible. After a time, QMC Terwilliger asked if he could join me. As space was at a premium, I quickly agreed.

I still remember our talk. "Tough day out there," said the chief.

Me: "Yes, it sure was."

Chief: "I guess you never expected to see that kind of action when you joined up?" I wasn't sure how to treat that question. It was probably rhetorical and I could say nothing. Or, I could say I had volunteered for duty in Viet Nam and that carried an expectation of exposure to some degree of risk. Instead, I decided to answer the way he probably wanted.

"No, not really," I said, "But then again, I wasn't that certain what I was getting into. My father was in the Navy during the Second World War. He advised me to join the Coast Guard. It seemed to make sense, so I joined. What about you?"

He thought for a few seconds, then, "My father was in the Guard. I never expected to get to Nam. But, once we were here, it seemed kind of almost inevitable that we would see some action. This is such a crazy war. All those protestors at home aren't completely wrong about this war."

I asked, "Where's your father now?"

"Dead." I was sorry I asked.

But he said, "That's alright. He's been dead a long time.

I only remember seeing him once when I was a kid. You don't want to hear this..."

Me: "Sure, I do. Go ahead."

"I lived with my grandparents. My Grandad was a BMCM when he retired from the Guard. They moved West then. My father was a Coastie lifer too. That's how my grandparents met him when he was a seaman striker. He was half Mexican. There weren't many Mexicans in the Guard then. Hell, not even now. They married, but my Mom died when I was born.

Staying with my Grandparents was all we could do. My Dad was a BM2 on board the Hamilton. My Granddad was on the Spencer. Both high endurance cutters, built in the '30's. Pride of the Coast Guard, they were." He stopped.

Me: "How long was your grandfather on board the Spencer?"

"From '41 until the very end," Terwilliger replied.

"Keep going, please."

"Why?"

"The Spencer fished my Dad out of the North Atlantic after his second DE was torpedoed."

"Small world." He offered me a cigarette. "I was two and a half when I saw my Dad leave.

He was on the Hamilton on convoy duty. Same as yours- North Atlantic.

She took a hit from a torpedo and went down in less than a minute according to the reports. No survivors! No wreckage! Nothing...The Germans .... The Nazis!"

The chief got up and left. To my surprise he was back in a minute or so with 2 cups of black coffee and cigarettes. He offered. I didn't smoke, but I took one anyway.

Me: "Is it because your Father and Grandfather were career that you joined up?"

"That, and the fact that after 25 or 30 years you can retire and

still be a fairly young man. The job and the life are fairly interesting. Of course, you have to like the sea. There aren't a lot of
shore billets for boatswain's mates, but I wouldn't have it any
other way."

"How about marriage?"

"That's the hard part. Hard to find the right girl. I've seen a
lot of bad things happen when guys are away, particularly on
long deployments. No. I'll wait until I retire. Sometime after I'm
40. Find the right girl. Get married and settle down on my
grandparents' avocado farm. Anyone waiting for you?"

I thought of Mollie, but answered, "No."

Flashes of pyrotechnics from near the shoreline brought our
talk to a halt. Point Arena rode past a world at war. For the moment, those of us aboard her were at peace.

20

TO SAUSALITO: NAVY SEALS

After delivering the Marines to DaNang, Point Arena needed a brief overhaul at Cam Rhan Bay before resuming its patrol duty. While underway, the crew was given a week's Rest and Relaxation (R&R). 50% of us had to be on hand to supervise repairs and answer questions. The CO said he would stay. I elected to go to Honolulu and stay at Fort De Russy- a mistake. First, it took a full day each way, leaving only 5 days there: and second, everyone there was married. Essentially alone for 5 days, I walked the beach, got more of a tan, and drank too much. I would need a better plan next time.

After repairs were completed, which included a bit of resurfacing the bullet damaged areas, we returned to our patrol waters between A-8 and A-12. (Point Leopard spent a great deal of time in dry dock.) Patrols went by for weeks with minor activity, but nothing to match the action with the Marines. Fewer weapons were being found. Fewer sampans went fishing. The war seemed to grow worse, but the level of involvement for the Point Arena was slowing. No one wished for more, but the hands began to discuss the lack of activity. I did not like the idea of tempting the Fates!

A few nights went by. Just after dark RM Ginger appeared on the bridge with a message he had decoded from USCGC Spencer, our mother cutter 5 miles offshore and laying off A-6. We were instructed to proceed under complete blackout to a specific point just north of A-12, stand-by 300 yards offshore and to await contact there. Arrival time was 0500.

LT Stone instructed QMC Terwilliger and me to assure that

Point Arena showed absolutely no light. We understood. The rendezvous point was perilously close to, if not in, North Viet Nam's territorial waters. (Even though the ANVN had a very small sea presence, it still might inflict real damage on an essentially unarmored cutter like Point Arena.)

We proceeded quietly and in total blackout mode. The night was now moonless with some low scudding clouds. An increasing wind created a bit of a small white caps. Point Arena might easily be mistaken for junk on ANVN radar. A second message appeared on the bridge and urged us to be 2 miles further north for the rendezvous at the same time. This definitively put us in enemy water. We arrived on schedule. Binoculars scanned the coastline and the waters to the north of our position. Nothing there!

Point Arena began the final maneuver to within 300 yards of shore. This made us extremely vulnerable. We saw nothing scanning ahead and abeam. The night was cool. Chief Terwilliger was at the bow. The cutter was slowing. Nothing insight. We arrived at 0450. Engines idling: we came to a dead stop.

Words rasped on the pregnant air, "Pull me up." At the ship's ladder, a form emerged from the black water and Peterson helped him aboard. The man was in a wet suit. He pulled off fins and kept moving on board. He was followed by seven others. Two men were Asians. Their hands were bound and they were gagged.

I was on the main deck in seconds. He pulled off his hood, saying, "My name's Pat Lynch, Mission Leader, Seal Team 5. This mission is highly classified. Are you the CO?" We set off to see LT Stone (recently promoted.). We were to take the Seal team and its prisoners to the nearest secure vessel. That seemed to mean Spencer, which was quickly confirmed by Ginger. We got underway immediately, running as silently as possible moving away from the coast on a generally southerly course that would have us intersect with Spencer at 0830.

After seeing that the prisoners were secured. I went to the galley where Lynch was having coffee. A quick survey showed a big man: as tall as me at 6"5", but wider in the shoulders and narrower in the hips, he appeared to be incredibly fit. I sat across from him. He put out a hand and said, "LT Pat Lynch, US Navy."

I responded, "LTJG Ronan O'Neill, US Coast Guard Reserve. XO. How did you all get those prisoners to the meeting point without being seen or heard?"

Lynch: "We took them at their encampment a few miles inland. They're both ANVN officers associated with communications. Some of us are a bit proficient in Vietnamese. They quickly understood that failure to cooperate would go poorly for them. We have not debriefed them. That's for experts. We brought them to the shore and had no real problem getting them to use their feet to kick once they got in deep water. That's about it. Oh! We don't make noise in the water."

I was impressed. "Wow!" was as good as I could do...

Lynch said back, "Fact is I never expected we'd get picked up by the Coast Guard. You all did very well."

"Do you do this often?"

Lynch: "Not every day. Not our first time either. But, if you do it all the time, then they would start to look for us and up their security in their home areas."

Me: "Seems like you could do some very decisive missions if ordered."

Lynch: "No doubt. Did you ever read 1984?"

Me: "Sure. Orwell."

Lynch: "This war's like that book. It's like Korea. There'll be no winner. It's part of the Communist containment policy. South Viet Nam is the surrogate for the United States and its allies. North Viet Nan is the same for China and Russia. One side starts to win, the other gets more resources from its backers. At some point, the peace process will get started and it will be just like

Korea. Thousands dead and no real winner."

Before I could respond, Peterson broke in, "We're coming up on the Spencer, gentlemen."

Lynch responded, "Nice meeting you, Ronan. After this, if you're in the San Diego area, drop in and see me at Coronado Island, home of the Seals."

21

TO SAUSALITO: A-12

What Lynch the Seal had failed to tell us was that the ANVN troop concentrations just north of the DMZ were the spearhead of an offensive that started just days after we delivered The Seals and their prisoners to the Spencer. Combat lasting about 2 months ensued-not the usual guerilla warfare, but armed combat with tanks and artillery on both sides. Ground was lost in the surprise offensive, but the U.S. Army and Marines began to rally and push north, slowly reclaiming territory lost at the outset of this struggle.

Point Arena played a role in some of these events. It provided fire support, as much as it could, and evacuation assistance for the Marines. It was present for quite a bit of action, was fired on and hit on several occasions, but no one was injured. The struggle was tedious, and after weeks of this fragmented action, all of the combatants seemed exhausted. Then it all appeared to end and Point Arena went back to her patrols between A-8 and A-12.

On a night in early July, LT Stone decided to take up a position about 800 yards south of a point in the northern area of A-12. On this moonlit night, any sampan or junk turning the point would be readily seen by the cutter's lookouts. Nothing appeared that night.

As day was breaking, BM2 Peterson and I were finishing our 4 hour watch. QMC Terwilliger came up the ladder to the bridge to relieve me. At the moment the chief stepped onto the bridge, Peterson said, "Something coming around the point."

I picked up my binoculars and saw a motorized junk with no numbering. I called LT Stone on the intercom. He advised to proceed to intercept. I gave the appropriate commands and sounded battle stations for security purposes. This was not a small junk. Our 50 and 20 cal. guns were all manned. I continued to watch the junk which was coming right for us. At about 500 yards, the junk's crew pulled a tarp off of what had looked like cargo on the forward deck to reveal a deck gun of significant size (relative to the Point Arena and her armament). I ordered all weapons to open fire and called LT Stone to the bridge ASAP. When he appeared, I said "Suggest we run?"

"Concur," he said and I gave the order to reverse course. He told RM3 Ginger to report to the Spencer and COMNAVOPS, and to ask for help. Then a trawler appeared around the point. Unlike the junk, it was moving faster than Point Arena. It too had deck guns. Almost on our seeing it, the trawler opened fire. I was moving off the bridge to fire control when a shell hit. The starboard side of the bridge was torn open. I went around to the port door and entered.

Stone was lying in a most unnatural position and I quickly realized that his right arm was missing up into his torso. Peterson was pulling himself back to the wheel which seemed functional. He clung to it and somehow maintained course. Chief Terwilliger was against the bridge bulkhead. He was bleeding profusely from a leg and his torso. I called for CM2 Foreman. I called down to the engine room to ENC Staller and told him, "Chief, we need all those engines can give us, or we won't be around very long!"

Point Arena sprang forward. We began to separate, albeit slowly, from the trawler. (At this point it was obvious: the junk had been a decoy; and, it worked.) The trawler continued to fire. The sounds of the trawler's guns were ominous. Near misses rocked the cutter. I left the bridge to do a quick survey of damage. Point Arena had sustained a second hit.

GM1Rafftery and SN Capelli laid in a grotesque heap near the remains of the .50 Cal and 81 mm machine gun/mortar twin mount. BMI Jacobsen, bleeding from his left arm, fired the star-board 20 Cal with his right arm to aim and right hand on the trigger. He was a sight I shall never forget!

As the distance between the vessels slowly increased, I told Peterson to zig-zag randomly. I checked with the ENC and he told me we had nothing left for speed. I turned to Terwilliger. Foreman, our corpsman, was doing his best. He seemed to have the leg wound stopped, but the torso wound was not cooperating. Terwilliger looked up at me. I said, "How you doin', chief? Hang in there!"

His face was ashen and his breathing ragged. He tried to talk and at first nothing came out. His head bowed and my stomach did a flip-flop. But then, his head came up. Foreman was trying furiously to staunch the flow. The chief looked me in the eye. He said, "No more. I'm done. Sure wish I had found that right girl." He died right then. I almost threw up on the spot.

Jacobson had stopped firing and Foreman was attending him.

"Can I look at your face and shoulder, Mr. O'Neill?" asked Foreman. Up to that moment, I was completely unaware that I was bleeding. Both sections of my right arm must have taken shrapnel. I could feel blood on my face, but did not know the source of the blood. After Foreman stopped the bleeding, I told him to go back to looking after Jacobsen at his 20 cal.

Two more near misses, then a new sound. Overhead, Navy jets dove at the trawler and hit it with several pieces of ordnance as well as cannon fire. The trawler stopped dead in the water. I panned around the horizon with my binoculars. The junk was heading back north. From the west/southwest, just visible over the horizon was the Spencer. I called the engine room, saying, "Reduce speed to 5 knots," and to Peterson, "Come to 2-5-0. The Spencer approaching. After we come about, I proceeded toward her by dead reckoning."

I slid down onto the deck, looked at Chief Terwilliger, then

LT Stone and I began to tear up for a few seconds. Then I got up and went to the left wing of the bridge. All that was left on the right was the .20 cal. mount. Peterson had stopped firing and Foreman was still attending his wounds. The Spencer was approaching at flank speed to rescue another O'Neill.

22

TO SAUSALITO
—USCGC SPENCER/SUBIC BAY

Everything was fuzzy when I awoke. The bed was strange as were the quarters. I felt the rolling of a ship, but knew it was not the Point Arena. A man was sitting not far away. I tried to ask him a question, but a strange series of sounds came out instead. His head snapped to attention. He stood, looked down at me and said, "Please, Don't move.

PLEASE!!" Then he was gone.

In a few minutes, another man appeared wearing a doctor's white smock and a name tag that said, "Harry Wartnick, M.D." Small initials appeared at the end of the name tag- unreadable at my distance. He looked down at me and identified himself. Took my pulse and asked the other man, "Erdman, please take the LT's blood pressure."

"130/79," said Erdman. The doctor said they were both U.S. Public Health Service, assigned to USCGC Spencer for her tour. He was the only doctor on board, but he was trained in trauma and emergency care.

"You will be fine in a month or two, LT, but I do not expect you will be seeing any further action for quite awhile. As soon as advisable, we will have you airlifted to Subic Bay for further analysis and then onto Hawaii for final recovery." It took a few seconds for me to process this news.

"How is everyone else?" was my response. He looked down and shook his head from side to side.

"Please, doctor, I saw some of them. I know LT Stone is dead. I was trying to treat Chief Terwilliger when he died. I really need to know, now, about the others. Please."

He pulled over the stool on which Erdman had been sitting when I awoke. LT Son is dead. So are GM Rafftery and ET Jones. BM Peterson and CM Forester are wounded, neither as seriously as you. And, but for the major blood and tissue losses, your wounds would not have been so bad. The shrapnel did not come out as well as I would have liked. BM Jacobson's wounds were very serious and he is at Cam Rhan Bay. Ginger had minor wounds and is up and about. Chief Staller and Capelli are fine. They all have asked about you repeatedly. When you are ready, I will let those who can do so visit you. Later, you can visit the others who are not ambulatory."

It took seconds for me to process this news. Then I asked, "Where are the bodies?"

"LT Son was turned over to ARVN. LT Stone is being sent back to the States. The other three are being buried at sea at 1400." The Doc looked at his watch, adding, "In less than 2 hours. Now lay back. We'll get some food in you. You'll feel stronger once you eat."

"Good," I responded," because I want to see my fellow crew men buried."

***

Four days later I was helicoptered to Subic Bay. As soon as I arrived, They went over my wounds, did more tests, had me do movements, and generally poured over me. I was quickly fully ambulatory, but exceedingly weak. They said I would go to Hawaii as soon as my orders were cut.

The next day I was asked to put on a uniform which fit me not so well. They were tropical whites, my favorite. I said the shoulder boards were wrong as I had 2 full stripes instead of the LTJG stripe and a half. But I was told I was wrong and there were no JG stripes handy anyway. As soon as I was dressed, A Commander stepped into my room and ordered, "Attention.

Admiral on board!"

The two corpsmen and I snapped to attention. Admiral Mc-Cain wheeled into the room followed by a LT. All three officers were Navy. CAPT Vaughn, skipper of the Spencer appeared last.

The Admiral stood in front of me, saluted and began to speak. I was overwhelmed but tried to keep up. Things were said about by order of the President I was promoted to LT, that I had performed above and beyond that to be expected of a ship out gunned and outmanned, that I had risked my life for the crew, and that I was herewith awarded the highest US Navy combat award, the Silver Star, and numerous other medals and decorations from the USCG as well as the government of South Viet Nam. It was all almost beyond comprehension.

When the Admiral finished, He looked at me as if I should speak. So I asked, "What about the crew and LT Stone?"

He looked at me and said," Somehow, I'm not surprised that would be the first thing you would ask. There are plenty of awards and commendations to go around to all. But you, LT, you were the only person on board Point Arena who was praised by every member of the crew. Congratulations, enjoy your time in Hawaii and I wish you a complete recovery. God speed."

23

CAROLYN — A RELATIONSHIP?

Before leaving for law school, I had learned that Tinker and Elaine, being engaged, were planning on moving in together. Tinker assured me that this would not interfere in my rooming with him (them). That concept made me uncomfortable. I hinted very clearly that as a concept, I did not think that would work out terribly well. Tinker hinted, discretely, that Sandra would need a roommate. I was very certain that I was not ready for that. (I believed that rooming with a woman almost absolutely assured a sexual relationship, and in Sandra's case that would doubtless turn serious.) So, I was getting to Sausalito with a very loose plan of having to find a place to live, but no real idea where, or by when, for that matter.

Crossing the Golden Gate brought a rush! I remembered just six months ago when I first made that trip. Getting off US 101 at Alexander and following that winding road down to the Cote d'Azur conjured the memory of the blonde woman on her mountain bike. I pulled onto the rooftop parking lot. There she was! She was hoisting her bike onto the rack on the back of her car. I got out. She looked my way and began to walk over. Our eyes met. She put her arms around my neck, saying, "It's been awhile, stranger. Where's your uniform?"

I bent ever so little and we kissed, deeply. I said, "We are both bad about writing, but I'm here now. How about you?"

She told me she had a shoot in Florida in 8 days, and she needed to be in shape. She was getting a chance to be in the Sports Illustrated Swimsuit issue. "WOW!" was all I could think to say. She asked how long I was planning to stay, so I told her about law school. She became very interested and asked where I planned to live. When I told her about Tinker and Elaine (but not Sandra), her eyes lit up. "My roommate is leaving on Monday. She got a great offer and is moving to Paris where she plans to be based for at least a year. I need someone right away to be able to stay on here. It's not really about the money. She's 23. I'm only 19, so I will need someone at least 21 on the lease with me. I know this is sudden, but it's like Kismet that you appeared out of nowhere when I needed someone." (I still remember those words as if she said them yesterday. I should. They changed my life in many ways.)

My response, "I'll think about it. What are the details?" Carolyn explained. Even the rent was not that bad. She ended with, "Look, I'll be away a lot. You know what I do. Almost all of my work right now is in California, but if this upcoming shoot pans out, that may change. You would have the place to yourself most of the time. And look: I won't be having many big parties and very few overnight visitors." With those last words, she looked into my eyes, and said, "Maybe none, depending on you."

"Can we talk tomorrow?" was the best I could do. I knew Tinker and Elaine were planning for me to go out with them and Sandy that night. Carolyn acquiesced and suggested lunch at her place. I agreed.

***

The next day, I was at her door at noon. She looked great - just a bit of make-up, cute shorts, low heeled sandals and a sort of red halter top. Her dirty blonde shoulder length hair was tied back in a pony tail. We went out on her deck. On the way, I saw all kinds of suitcases and boxes. It certainly looked like her roommate was leaving. "Will you miss her?" I asked.

"More than you'll ever know and more than I'll probably ever be able to put into words," was her response and she stopped it there. She pointed to a chair and I sat. She offered me a glass of what looked like iced tea and I nodded, so she poured-first me, then her. Then she reached down next to her and pulled out some papers.

"Here's what the landlord wants to get signed," as she handed the papers to me. It was a lease in my name for one year. Carolyn's name was not on it. I was stunned. Then after a moment I realized that since she was 19, she could not sign as in California she was technically a minor. It was not a long document but the print was very small. I had never seen a California lease, but it didn't look that different to me from those in Maryland and D.C.

"It's a lot of money when you look at a whole year," I said.

"I know," was all she said and with that handed me an envelope. I opened it. Inside was cash. I counted it:

$4,800!

"WOW!" was all I managed.

"This way, you have half the rent money for the whole year. Six months or so after that, I'll be 21 and we can get the lease redone in my name. And remember, this place is barely furnished. Lisa doesn't care and most of it is mine. I 'll trust you with it. But I will want Lisa's room. You can have her bed. I'm quite fond of my own. What do you say?"

I was frankly amazed by her plan. There seemed so little risk. Sandra might not like it, but with Carolyn gone so often, they might never meet. I looked at Carolyn. She looked in my eyes. I could tell she wanted this. Maybe she wanted me? Tinker thought it might work, but he didn't know about the lease. I thought for a second and decided. This building, Sausalito, the view - all of these and more - were reasons I wanted to live in this Bay Area. Here it all was — on a platter and it solved the Tinker/Elaine dilemma too. So, with my blinders closely affixed, I said, "How can I say no? Of course, I'll do it."

She handed me a pen, I signed and it was done. That fast!

"How about we celebrate?" Carolyn said, beaming her smile at me. When I nodded, she produced two glasses and presented me with a bottle of Champaign. I opened it and handed it to her. She poured. We clicked glasses. Our eyes locked! We drank.

"How about we celebrate more inside?' She said as she stood, took my free hand and steered me through the boxes and other packing toward an interior room. We were in her bedroom. She sat her drink down. With one hand she freed her hair. With the other, the halter top. In seconds, I was in her arms and she was kissing me passionately. She helped me with my clothes. We were on her bed, kissing, then touching, and then Carolyn took charge.

***

Some time later, she stared down at me. I was exhausted, but so pleased physically. Months ago, when we had made love, I had been drinking. This time not. I looked at her. Carolyn was not a wisp of a woman. She was tall, long and lightly muscled, and not really soft —- athletic, very athletic. She took the lead and knew what she wanted and how to go about it. At that moment I had a thought: how does a 19 year old know all of this? Heck, I didn't know virtually any of it.

Like she read my mind, which she would do often in the times to come, she said, "You're only the second man I have ever been with. That first man I was with only twice. We did only what he wanted. I did not like that he seemed intensely selfish. You are so much a man that you don't need to be in charge every second. I like that. I really do. When Lisa leaves, my mentor leaves. She taught me so much. But I know that I still have so much to learn. I hope you'll help me." Her eyes rested on mine. They were alive with life. I had no sense that she loved me. It was like I was an alien person that Carolyn had discovered on her own and now she wanted to explore me, or be with me.

Turns out I was right, way more right than I would come to learn for a long while!

24

SANDRA

Once, during my first year of law school, I had the opportunity to watch Sandra deal with a difficult situation. (Please understand that after your first year all class schedules are *ad hoc* in make-up with sign-ups and class availability governed by a complex set of rules.) Sandra had put together a demanding track during her second year at Hastings. She wanted to be considered for a Supreme Court clerkship (California would do, but she wanted the big plum in D. C). To do that she needed a broad array of difficult subjects, including some seminars which could conflict if put off to her third year when she planned to get a judicial internship with her father's influence being a big factor.

Accordingly, she had arranged her schedule with great care to accommodate all of the needed commitments over the course of her first 2 years and the first semester of her 3rd.

At the end of the first semester, Professor Schwartzman, who presided over a seminar on First Amendment rights and duties became ill. To accommodate her needs, Sandra needed to take a substitute seminar. Only problem was it was full. She knew some of those enrolled. None were willing to give it up. She asked my advice and I suggested she ask the others (total of only 12!). She thought on that and called her father. Then she typed a note, copied it 6 times and stuffed 7 envelopes. The next day she put them in mail slots. That night she had three calls. The next day she told me she was in the new seminar on First Amendment rights.

That next weekend, we had some time together alone. I asked

her how she had done it. Sandra said, "I built on your idea. Everyone in that class needs that seminar. Even my best smile wouldn't budge them. I was sure of that. So, I asked my Dad to fund my predicament. Then, I offered to pay $500 to the first person to give me their seat. I had three takers. The person who sold it to me got back in for $250. I won. That's all I cared about."

As I write this, I think about Sandra a great deal. I spent a large part of three years of my life with her. There were signposts along the way, yellow flags like this one saying that she was single-minded, but no red flag until that last fateful day.

25

SANDRA AS A FUTURE LAWYER

In all of the discussions we have had about the people in my life, Sandra is the one person whom I remain terribly uncertain about how to address my feelings toward her. Once and for a few years, I saw her as my potential spouse and mother of my children. However, I was never able to come to grips with her family, and especially how she related to them. (Another instance, like Mollie, where it seemed "something was missing.")

My first year of law school and then a summer clerkship with her father's firm went reasonably well. We spent vast amounts of time together, but since Sandra had a strict code of behavior and lived at home, we shared little intimacy or real affection (thank goodness for Carolyn). Most of our time was spent on social occasions as we both had serious amounts of work from law school and our part time clerking duties at the firm. As Sandra was a year ahead of me, typically she would have to worry about securing a job. But not with her father's firm and she did appear to have all the qualifications and talent needed for long term success (smart as shown by high grades, verbal having won an award in moot court, and highly motivated for success - she rejected a lower appellate judicial clerkship to start her career at the Firm).

Sandra seemed to have me as part of her life's plan. At times, I began to develop the sense that I was seen as the perfect adjunct to this perfect woman. Did this make me jealous, or even uncomfortable? Not at first; but, over time, it began to feel more and more that way, particularly in combination with other factors involving the family Firm.

During my second year, I took a position as a part time clerk at the Firm. This was more stressful than I realized going in caused by any number of my assignments having deadlines that did not seem consistent with a part time research clerk. Nonetheless, and especially because of my relationship to Sandra, I spent the time and made the effort to finish every project in a timely manner. Not all of those assigning work provided me with feedback. Some critiques seemed unnecessarily harsh going to a second year law student. Moreover, the junior partner assigned as my mentor rarely could make time to provide advice or feedback. In all, the experience was more than a bit bizarre.

When I went to mention this seeming disconnect that I was experiencing at times to Sandra, I was more than a bit taken aback by her reaction: something like-we cannot discuss assignments from others unless there is a need to know basis. This seemed strange since I wanted to talk about the workings of the firm, not the substantive research issues. No matter: this turned into a dead end street as something to discuss with Sandra.

The good news was that my overall evaluation was high and I was welcomed as a summer clerk. This firm program had a mid-level partner in charge and half a dozen junior partners with active mentoring roles. I was treated quite differently than I was during the school year. Since I was older and more of a known asset, I was given more difficult assignments. And because of my almost year of research and writing clerkship, I was able to complete them quickly, efficiently and accurately. With a few weeks to go in the summer, Sandra's father called me into his office.

He seemed more casual than usual and had another partner present. I sensed a pending problem. Wrong! "Ronan, we are exceptionally pleased with your work. As an older clerk during the year, we were able to observe that you were very resourceful and effective. This summer, you have been far and away the leading clerk. We see no reason to wait on the completion of the summer program. We are offering you an associateship when you graduate and a clerkship for one semester of your choice during your third year so that you can take an active internship of your choosing during the other semester. By the way, you are only the fourth clerk ever to receive this offer. Congratulations!"

Of course, I accepted on the spot. That was my high point while at "The Family Firm."

26

CAROLYN'S RETURN

As my venture with Sandra moved forward, my relationship with Carolyn seemed to change, almost by imperceptible degrees. We spent less time together. But since Sandra was not into cohabitation, I was able to maintain a degree of personal privacy under a rubric that my apartment mate only allowed me and not guests as that person was the tenured prime tenant (interestingly, a position which Sandra seemed to accept, and hold, not only as satisfactory, but almost as an article of faith.)

Over the months during Sandra's second year, my first, this worked well for both of us. I needed the high first year grades to make law review, and Sandra had some difficult second year courses, including Evidence, Constitutional Law, and the most consuming of all, Richard Powell (an archetypical model for the Paper Chase - brilliant, groundbreaking, eccentric and in his mid-80s, one of the Old Lions of the Faculty) for Trusts, Wills and Estates. I had the other Lion for Torts, Prosser himself. As such, we needed vast amounts of time for our studies.

Carolyn had advanced to modeling in Europe, the Caribbean, and other glamour spots. She told me she would be in the next Sports Illustrated Swimsuit edition on the back of a postcard from Bimini. Then one night, as my enthusiasm for reading footnotes was waning, I heard a bump against the front door and went to check. There she stood in a February drizzle, dark with a gorgeous tan and hair almost white from sun exposure, swathed in raingear of a sort and holding packages. With a warm smile, Carolyn said in a low voice, "Please let me in. I'm wet, tired, and I want someone I can trust to talk with."

Stepping aside she slid in while handing me a package as I said, "Well, Hello. Delighted to see you. But this is a bit of a surprise. I somehow did not expect you."

"Oh, afraid I mailed you a note yesterday from New York, and I beat it home. Here, please help me out of these wet things. Would you grab my roll bag, it's right outside the door. I shipped everything else." And with that she took the package from me, looked at it carefully and exchanged it for another.

"Here, open this one first." I did, and it contained a pair of shiny pants with zippers on the lower leg and an elastic waist. "It's French exercise wear. I loved the fabric and thought it would look great on you. Now open this one."

I complied. It was a top to match the bottom. "Thank you," I said.

"Let's see how they fit?" half a question, half a command as she said it. With that Carolyn turned, passed through the doorway to her bedroom and flipped on her lights. "Come on in. I won't bite."

I complied. She had on a similar outfit under her rain gear. She looked at me, up and down and paused with her eyes on my belt buckle, "Well?"

I started to take my pants off. Carolyn said quite nonchalantly, "I haven't been with a man since the last time with you." And with that she pulled her top over her head to reveal nothing but herself. As I finished, she kept looking at me with a somewhat bemused expression on her face.

"You're not hard," said in a disappointing voice.

"This is all kind of sudden" from me.

"Does your girlfriend keep you fully satisfied," was her retort.

"Let's keep her off limits."

"OK. Do you want to finish?"

Her face was uncertain. I thought for half a second, "Yes."

I took off my top as she took off her bottom. She was tan everywhere. She had no pubic hair! In a husky voice, Carolyn said, "I've been with all women the last four months. I've been thinking about a man. Thinking about you, for weeks now. Please make love to me, slow, boy-girl love. We'll try on your outfit when we're done." As I moved toward her, Carolyn's face broke into a radiant smile.

We made love for hours.

The outfit was a perfect gift!

27

MENKA'S

In the early Fall of my second year, Sandra asked me to take her for a special dinner to an unusual restaurant on the road into Point Reyes National Seashore. She assured me that we could take the scenic coastal road up to Point Reyes Station, and the more traditional highway, Sir Francis Drake Boulevard *back* to her apartment. I agreed. We had a fantastic drive, mindful of the opening sequences in Alfred Hitchcock's *The Birds*. The day was warm, breezy and sparkling. We stopped twice to walk in the sand, kissing longingly the second time. It was a bit before 6 p.m. when we arrived.

Menka's looked like a creation from a fairy tale. No 90 degree angles were noticeable. The finish changed all over the exterior. The windows held old leaded glass with diagonal iron criss-crossing to keep the panes in place. The lintel for most doors differed and they were of varying heights. The interior finish was more, though not completely, homogenous. While the trim was a brilliant array of colors seemingly never replicating itself. The tables and chairs were nineteenth century agrarian. Electricity seemed a surprise in this step back in time and place. Then came the menus: Russian and English. Boy, was I surprised!

Sandra ordered. Everything after the Borscht tasted a whole lot better than that soup (not meant as a compliment.). The saving grace was the vodka and the wine. By dessert, I was bit woozy. When we got almost to the car Sandra said, "I don't think you should drive.'

Taken a bit aback, I considered for a second before responding, "Do you feel comfortable driving my stick shift back?"

Without a pause, she said, "No. But while you were in the Men's, I checked and they have rooms. I reserved one. Why don't we spend the night?"

What could I say. Within minutes we were in a cabin almost as quaint as the restaurant. I drank a few glasses of water and felt a bit better. Sandra used the bathroom and returned in bra and panties. (I had seen as much in her bathing suits and there were two beds.) Besides which Sandra had been clear that she planned to save herself for her wedding night ("Hooray" for Carolyn!). When she sat on the edge of her bed, she beckoned me to come over next to her. She helped me undress a bit. She stretched out and moved over, leaving room for me. I picked up on that signal. We kissed. We felt each other. We moved deeper into passion. Then, she separated herself, gently. She arched her back and pulled down her panties. She took my shoulder and moved my face down her body. Then, looking me in the eyes, Sandra said, "Please do me. I know you know so much more about sex than me. I don't want to wait until our wedding night for everything."

28

CAROLYN'S CAREER TAKES OFF

Over the random days and weeks that followed her sudden reappearance, I saw a fair amount of Carolyn. But it was not just as my apartment mate. Scanning a magazine stand, my gaze abruptly shifted back to a magazine called Glamour. Carolyn's face was staring at me from the cover. A few weeks later, I saw what appeared to be her again on the cover of Redbook which had appeared on our family coffee table since my memory started. So, finally I asked her, "Carolyn, I feel like I have seen your face on two magazine covers. Could that be you?"

Her head went down, then tilted up coyly, her eyes sparkling, "Yes. That's me. I had a pretty good run of luck while I was away."

"But I thought you were doing a bathing suit shoot?"

The same head and eye gestures were repeated, this time with a mischievous grin, "Well, we did a series of shots for Sports Illustrated in the Caribbean. The photographer liked me a lot with very few clothes on, so he asked me to come to New York with him for a high end lingerie shoot. That went well and one of its producers asked if I did things with clothes on. Kind of silly sounding now, but funny then. The next thing I knew, my agent had raised my rates twice and I was in real demand. There were 5 covers, I think. Sports illustrated got wind of what was happening. The Swimsuit producer called and I did another shoot. Next week when the magazine comes out, I'll be on the cover of that too. Like I said, pretty lucky! A real hot streak."

Frankly, I was stunned. Carolyn seemed pretty much the same young woman who had left for that bathing suit shoot. But now, it seemed she was a star of sorts. I was dumbfounded for more than a few seconds, then, "Does this mean you'll be moving back to New York? Or, somewhere else?"

"No. Don't be concerned. I have no plans to move. Our arrangement couldn't be better. You go to school, study and hang out in the City most of the time. I work out, relax, cycle, catch up with friends, see some of them, and from time to time, we get together. If you don't mind my asking, what do you tell your girlfriend about me?"

I knew this moment would have to come and had thought about a wide variety of responses, all rooted in the truth. Not knowing exactly what was going to come out, "Well, I have told her that my apartment mate is the senior person on the lease, gives me a good deal and has a few wishes that I must honor. First, no company. Quiet is a strong preference. Second, privacy is also paramount. That I see very little of my cotenant, and we both like it that way. That's about the gist of it."

Those words still stay with me after all these years. Carolyn asked, "Does she know I'm a woman?"

"No."

"So, there's no reason for her to be jealous as you've painted me as a bit of a recluse?"

I bowed my head and mumbled, "That's been my intention. I've wanted the best of both worlds. Was I wrong?"

Carolyn, "I'd have to say 'no.' After all, I want the best of many worlds, so who am I to criticize? But, I will admit to a bit of jealousy. I do wonder how she likes the way you make love? Some of the things I've taught you?"

I was in a bit of a quandary at that point, not wanting to get into Sandy and my relationship; still, "We are not at the same sexual point in our relationship." I stopped. Carolyn was beaming, almost laughing. In fact, I believe a giggle slipped out.

She grabbed me by the hand and pulled me toward her bedroom, happily saying, "It's high time I taught you some of the things I learned during my travels, especially in Paris!"

29

MY PACT WITH CAROLYN

Carolyn's modeling trips became more frequent. She said "Her Look" had caught on in the face of a fashion trend called the "natural movement," which was especially popular with the younger set, including the Hippy, or would be, types as well as with *haute couture* types who currently featured "a bit is more" look. Since she had changed little since I first encountered her, I thought Carolyn looked like the California girl next door. Whatever the reasons, she was in demand. She travelled first class, all over the world. She was lined up for the next Sports Illustrated, and had covers on Vogue and Vanity Fair. Her rates were among the highest and she had all sorts of side benefits. (Collaterally: Her manager had used their relationship to bring them both into New York's number one agency.)

Returning from one trip, she had something new: high grade marijuana. THAT made me nervous. Carolyn used it rarely and had a small amount. Still, this was more than a bit out of line with what I thought (other than her sexual appetite) made her so All-American. Plus, just possession of marijuana could undermine my legal career before it got off the ground. When I tried to discuss these factors with her, Carolyn was surprisingly resistant to even hear my views. In tum, this caused more concerns. That reunion ended with my saying I had to go study for a presentation tomorrow (it was really a few days away).

When I got back about 5 the next afternoon, Carolyn was at my bedroom door moments after I had put my books down. It was a Tuesday, The next day I had 4 classes for which to prep. The presentation was due at my only class Thursday afternoon.

When I called to her to come in, she opened the door, but did not cross the threshold. Standing there, hair tied back, little make-up, cutoffs and a loose T-top, Carolyn did not look like a world class model. She glanced downward and started, "You know, you are really the only man with whom I have had an adult relationship. You're older. You've been through so much. You have ambition. You are totally straight. So, I know in my heart, we'll never be a couple, a real couple. But here, when I get back, it's like you're my base, my home, my touchstone. I don't have anyone like you. I don't want anyone else. I love the way we are. I don't want it to change." She took two steps stopped a few feet away and looked me in the eyes, "I love you. I know it's a less than complete love, but still, it's more love than I have for anyone else."

I wasn't sure what to say, clearly, more than I knew went on behind that beautiful face, "You never said anything like that. Frankly I'm surprised, honored even. Why tell me all this now?"

Her eyes went down, she had wanted to hear more, maybe something else. Looking up, "For some reason, the way you went on about the dope caught me off guard and really hurt my feelings. I overreacted. I spent hours thinking about that, us, and where we are and where we are going and where we'll never go in our relationship. So, my declaration. And I'm sorry for the way I behaved last night."

My turn, "You know I'm incredibly fond of you. But you have been continuously honest about your primary sexual preference. Fair play. I don't want us to change. Do you?"

"Do you have to study?"

"Yes. Big day tomorrow- 4 classes. I do appreciate the apology!"

"Some quick make-up sex?"

Carolyn made dinner afterward so I could study. When I looked over once, I thought I saw tears running down her face, but she smiled all through the dinner chatting away as if the day before had never happened.

Each parting and *reunion after that, for years, tended to be joyous for both of us. We were mutually pleased with each other and our friendship with all of its benefits. I never told anyone the whole truth about my roommate. Over time, I remained most reluctant to discuss Carolyn with Dr. Arnaud or anyone else. Discretion always seemed to be the more prudent course in this area of my life, but if I could have learned not to act as I did in the first instance, that would have been far more discrete. This whole thought process, whenever repeated, made Dr. Arnaud more than a little displeased.*

30

CAROLYN'S LIFE KEEPS CHANGING

C arolyn was excited about her career and, as it turns out, about her new best girlfriend in New York. Her name was Violet. She was also a swimsuit model, but older than Carolyn. They had met on several shoots and first became friendly, and then one night after a few drinks, lovers.

Things progressed. Violet's roommate in Manhattan moved out of their rent control apartment. Carolyn moved in. Were they in love?

Carolyn was interesting when she got to that point. (None of this came out quickly, certainly not the way I am relating it here.) "Love" was not a word I remembered her using over those years, at least not regarding people as opposed to clothes, or especially shoes. It seemed her career and this relationship were what she wanted to talk about. We did so, on and off for a week (I had to study and clerk. She exercised and shopped.) We talked and made love. Nothing conclusive came of it.

She finally mentioned that Violet was French and had a place in Paris. Violet wanted her to spend time there with her. Carolyn felt it might be way too much, too soon. PLUS, turns out Violet's English was OK; while Carolyn's French was not. I think the way things were addressed that Violet made considerably more money than Carolyn and that might be causing her a concern too.

So, I asked if she wanted me to take over the Cote d'Azur completely? This upset her. She said, "I thought you understood you are the only man I care about. I do not want to lose this relationship or have it get totally swallowed up by my career. I guess that's what I came back here to say."

This was one of the longest times we spent "together." (If you could call it that with classes, studying, clerkship and Sandra.) Looking back, I should have done a better job of getting to the bottom of what Carolyn was really about. For years after, I secretly felt I had somehow failed her. And, of course, I even wondered if I did love her in a way like no other person. (Of course too, as the years rolled by, I came to know that I did love her, very much!) Dr. Arnaud was very unhappy with me about my "honesty" in facing my feelings toward Carolyn. Yet, the good doctor never said what it was she wanted me to do or say about Carolyn, except to tell Mollie about her.

31

A FINAL STRAW

(NOTE: This chapter is a bit repetitious, yet I feel it needs to be said somewhere, so here it goes.)

Dr. Arnaud was always pursuing the reasons why I might have acted as I did that fateful day. Her pressure was neither insistent nor intense. Yet, I knew then that I had to figure all of this out, so I could come to grips with it, and myself, and get on with the bigger business of my life, like marriage and having children.

At an intellectual level, and for various reasons, I knew that Sandra, her family and the Firm, all played roles in shaping my behavior. I was able to relate to my lack of interest in working for her father and his intermediaries with whom he would have had me interact. I realized that telling Sandra that I did not want to be at the Firm might create some real problems with her. A real question was whether her father's reaction would be worse (and if it would hurt me in getting a job at a much smaller firm). So, I knew I had to tell Sandra first.

But the bigger issue was Sandra and her family and their whole social scene, especially on the San Francisco society stage. What this meant, in reality, was a probable wedge for me with her family. And yet, the Wedding date was bearing down on us. Invitations had been sent. I spent a bad day or two. We met at her place. Sandy poured us each a glass of her favorite white table wine. Small talk ensued. She picked up her glass and sat down next to me -very close. (I took this as a signal that Sandy wanted to be kissed or more.) I leaned over and kissed her. She responded very enthusiastically, but I could sense her waiting for me to initiate what would come next.

Ever since that night at Point Reyes, I had come to understand that when it came to our pre-marriage sex life, anything short of actual coitus was "on the table." So, my hand found its way inside her blouse. I rubbed downward on her stomach. I unbuttoned her slacks. Soon, we were in her favorite position, which I had learned to refine and intensify (with some advice from Carolyn). In a few minutes, she had climaxed. My needs, as was often the case, were put on hold.

She changed positions and she began to relax in my arms. I figured this was as good a time as any to mention the firm, "Sandra, I have something I need to tell you. I don't think it's something we will be able to discuss very easily. I have been vexed by this for quite a while." She pulled away, sat up and seemed ready to interject, but I quickly put an index finger to her lips, and continued, " It's your father's Firm. I just cannot go to work there when I have passed the Bar."

With that, she was on her feet instantly without my sensing her to have actually moved from next to me. Her first words looking down at me, uttered darkly and slowly were, "I cannot fucking believe what you just said!" And then, she really lost it!! Ranting and raving would not begin to convey how she acted. Her face was distorted and quickly became a mottled red with welts on her cheeks and forehead. After 10 minutes or so, I came to understand that I was literally not going to get a word in edgewise. I decided to leave. When Sandy realized that I was going, she only became more incensed, if that was possible. None of the words she was screaming at me were getting through: only her blind all encompassing wrath, or perhaps just an overpowering sense of hatred. So, I left. Sandra's last words rang in my ears, "You'll never work in San Francisco! NO ONE WILL HAVE YOU!!"

The next day when I reported to the firm, I was told to pick up my things in the Personnel Office. An envelope was hand delivered to me and I saw the assistant write a note to herself to that effect. Looked like this was not going to go smoothly. That was an understatement.

32

CHANGING RELATIONSHIPS

What follows are excerpts from two sessions with Dr. Arnaud.

Mollie and my mother became close friends. Mom, despite her involvement in D.C. and its many activities, missed Philadelphia. She went to visit often, but once her parents passed, and they did so surprisingly close together, she had lost her primary place to stay as the family home was to be sold for the benefit of her siblings. In the month or so after her mother passed, she needed to be in Philadelphia, happened to be talking to Mollie and was invited to stay at their home in Mount Airey. Mollie's mother had passed. They went to dinner with Mollie's dad as a threesome. My mother's interest in the family home increased and she persuaded her siblings to let her buy it at fair market value to allow her to move back to her home town, or at least to have a base there. Over time, Mollie's Dad and my Mom became close, very close.

Because of Mom, I was somewhat continuously aware of Mollie. I saw her twice on two different Christmas visits to Philadelphia. She was more beautiful, self-possessed and interesting than when I had left for law school. She was a systems analyst for IBM, worked from Center City, but spent a great deal of her time out and about working with clients and coworkers. That last Christmas of my third law school year, when we spoke, and we were still friends, she seemed a bit more distant, but she remained friendly and I thought she might still care about me. But then I flew back to the City and school, my clerk job, my future after law school, with Carolyn, and when was I going to propose to Sandra soon as everyone, especially her parents thought I would, so we could marry soon after graduation, Mollie quickly vanished from my thoughts. A month passed, I proposed. Sandy said YES. We started planning a wedding for right away after graduation, even before we knew if I would have passed the bar. During those days of my melt down, Mollie never entered my ever more confused thought processes.

Then, as I was there, standing on that Bridge railing, looking down, contemplating my mortality, and causing the beginning of a traffic jam, I heard a feint voice. Somehow slightly familiar, a voice was calling my name, repeatedly louder and with intensifying urgency each time, "Ronan! Ronan! Don't! DON'T, RONAN!!

Then, I looked down and out on the decking, there running toward me was Mollie. I froze first: surprised! Without thinking, I began to climb down. She reached me and grabbed my hand, pulling me. We started to run in the direction from which she had come. We got in her car. We drove past mine. We did not talk. When we had finished crossing the Golden Gate Bridge, she made a couple of quick turns and headed back to the City. At the end of Doyle Drive, Mollie said, "What the Hell were you doing?" My head went down and I started to cry.

When we got to her hotel, she took me right to her room. She showed me the bathroom and said matter of factly, "Please wash your face and get ahold of yourself."

I did as she bid. Upon returning, she stared at me, "Your Mom gave me your address in Sausalito. I was coming to see you to tell you that my Dad and your Mom have decided to get married. She asked me to do that because of how very fond you were of your father. NOW, what am I going to tell her?"

After sitting there for silent moments, "I was just standing on that rail thinking. I had only been there for a few minutes. I was looking for a way to go forward. I couldn't think of one. So many things were not going the way I planned for them to go. I was crushed, confused and felt entangled to a point of no escape.

Frankly, I was beyond despondent. It had all been building for days. I felt so utterly alone. I had no one whom I could trust to talk out all of my issues."

Mollie, "You have my attention. Go ahead. Talk!"

So, I did.

When I finished, I had talked for a long while. Mollie never interrupted. She looked at me steadily, but not unkindly. Then, "So, what happens next?"

Me: "I don't know."

A few moments passed, then, "Let's talk it through. Are you going to try that again anytime soon?"

She ordered room service. We talked for hours. I called the SFPD and told them my car stalled on the bridge. They told me it would cost me $430 to get it back and that I needed to talk to the Golden Gate Bridge District police first. I asked if that could wait a day or two. No problem.

Mollie said, "I think you need to get some rest. Can you sleep on my bed and I'll sleep in the chair?"

I looked at her, "Would you sleep with me? I need someone to hug in the worst way."

Next day, we had a plan. Mollie called my Mom and told her I was not well when she arrived, that she had not told me about her father's proposal, and that she was going to stay on until I was on my feet. The day after, I did my introductory interview with you and got my car. Later that same day, you agreed to take me as a patient. The next day, I told Sandra's father that I would not be accepting the associate position with his firm. That same night, I told Sandra that our relationship had ended, that I was very troubled, and needed time.

I had gone to Sausalito and got a suitcase of clothes. There was a note from Carolyn to say she was gone to the Caribbean for a week or two for a shoot and to check the refrigerator. I had omitted any detailed discussion of my roommate in being forth-coming with Mollie. She had left cold Chinese. I left it and went back to Mollie in the City. When I got to her room, I asked, "How long can you stay?"

When she hesitated, I said, "I don't want you to go." She looked back at me in the same way she had when I was pouring my heart out over the last two days.

"Ronan, I don't have to go back right away. IBM is everywhere. But why? Do you want me here?"

That first real moment of clarity came and I said, "Mollie, I finally realized: it is you that I love. None of these other women are you. You understand people. You understand me. You really seem to actually care. I know you once loved me. I don't know how you feel about me now."

She stood up, put out her hand to me, and said, "Come to bed with me. It's you I've always wanted."

My mother never heard about the Bridge railing, she only heard that Mollie and I were going to be married. I declared myself fine, but I still had, and continue to have, doubts about myself and a continuing sense of uncertainty. Mollie is a marvelous wife, mother, systems analyst and person.

Her coming back into my life, put me on the road to where we are today. I just wish I had been a better husband, even father, but I have been a damn good lawyer.

33

GETTING HELP: FIRST STEP

What follows is an excerpt from our first session. It says a lot about me, but not all. I still deal with that night in Pearl Harbor with Kate. I always will. And this is the first time I have written even a hint of it.

Tinker, Mollie, and especially you helped pull me back together after my breakdown was over. The first days are still a bit of a blur. I suspect it was the drugs, the racing, out of control emotions, and the recollection of the irreparable harm I could have inflicted on any number of people, most especially myself. So, this will be my first attempt to set out a record of what I then believed led me to the very cusp of contemplating that jump from the bridge.

More than any single factor was my sense that I was rushing out of control through a series of irreconcilable decisions: a potential marriage that I found all the more troubling with each day as it approached, a job that did not seem to be at all consistent with why I had gone to law school, people and loyalties that were slipping away- especially my family, Carolyn, and, not necessarily lastly, a marked concern that I had made too many seemingly irresponsible decisions from which there was no road back. One road that I did not see at all in my retrospective analysis was Mollie. Even then, within days I had come to see that I had taken Mollie for granted, even after I rejected her those years ago, and when, in reality, she was so very special and I had failed to appreciate her-at all for so very long!

Some marijuana and too much alcohol combined with these misgivings and words that were incredibly harsh and insensitive: all while heading back to Sausalito in a despairing state of mind. There, in this emotional swirl, my car somehow stopped, before I realized what I was doing, I was on that rail peering down. My mind was foggy, but I had not decided to jump, but I was considering it. Then, I heard that voice I had no way of expecting. It gave me pause. I looked down and there was Mollie, running toward me, screaming my name!

So, here I am. Tinker knows some things and says he understands and will stand by me. Mollie knows some things, certainly not all the same ones that Tinker knows or suspects. So, now, Dr. Arnaud, you know everything I know now. What I don't know is what I don't know; or, as you sometimes say, what I refuse to admit to myself. So, we are at this point. It's time to search for what's missing and that with which I must come to grips in order to move on with my life. I think I can do it, but I am not sure. This is hard, just me and your microphone. You told me you would explain later. I hope so. I still feel so lost. That's the best I can do for now.

34

MOLLIE: OUR RELATIONSHIP BEGINS TO FLOURISH

Another tape of a session.

Back in my life with moments to spare, Mollie seemed so changed. The years apart had changed her a bit physically —- she now had an aura that I was missing in the past. Mollie also had a physicality that simply was not there in days before.. Mollie radiated a persistent strength, confidence, even sensuality. In seemingly no time, I came to depend on her, to want to be with her, even to escape into her.

As you drew out of me overtime, I had come to see Mollie as my savior. Perhaps she was? I will never know if I would have jumped if her shout had not brought me back to a sense of reality. That said: I became firmly in her thrall. My attitude toward Mollie did not change as I began my recovery process. In fact, I became even more besotted. Came November: I passed the bar. Mollie had moved to San Francisco, having transferred with Big Blue. I had moved in with her on apart time basis. The California Bar results appeared and I passed. I had no job-not even a prospect. Then, Carolyn returned.

Our sessions had me feeling back to where I had some self-confidence and knew I had to begin to construct a future for myself. I could think about working, finally practicing law. But mostly, I had to close the door on Sandra, her family and her father's firm. And, once again, I had to decide about Mollie. That decision was now the easiest. The day after I passed the Bar, I called her father to seek his formal permission to ask her to marry me. Despite my problems, he readily agreed (I always suspected that road had been well paved before my call). Next,

I called my mother to tell her of my actual Decision (she was back in Philly). She was thrilled. She asked when I would ask Mollie. I hadn't gotten that far. She suggested two things: first that I give Mollie my maternal grandmother's engagement ring (to be reset according to Mollie's wishes); and, that I propose to Mollie on Thanksgiving in Philadelphia. I agreed to the first, but was reluctant on the second. Mostly, I wanted this to be about Mollie, me and our new life in the West.

So, in a moment of insight (proving to myself that I really was improving), I suggested a compromise: Mom could come to San Francisco as could Mollie's father, and I would propose here. Mom agreed. (I still needed to persuade Mollie about Thanksgiving.) When I suggested we invite the parents, Mollie agreed readily, and she insisted that she would prepare the Thanksgiving feast. Lastly, I invited Tinker and Elaine.

So it came to pass that on that Thanksgiving in 1974 that I proposed to my wife. Mollie said, "Yes." And we set a date in January to marry in San Francisco, honeymoon in Hawai'i, and have a reception in Chestnut Hill in the spring. The Tuesday before Thanksgiving I took my oath as a lawyer. We had a great weekend celebrating all of this. Mom stayed on for a few days to see "some people" in the Bay Area, but was noticeably absent until her **last** night in town. She was unusually happy. There were tears. The next day, I began to seriously look at firms where I could begin to be a trial lawyer.

Let me say that as the years have rolled by, these months have never been far from my mind. The pain, the mental devastation, the strange thought processes, that shout of my name, the salvation - all of it came to reveal the wholly positive side of Mollie. This was the beginning of a shared life. Mollie was my life, my co-parent, my inspiration, my wife.

35

AN EARLY FIRST DISCLOSURE

*D*r. Arnaud and Mollie were my lifelines following the mental and emotional tumult that lead up to the Bridge episode. Dr. Arnaud patiently explored how I had gotten myself into the state in which /found myself that day. Slowly and carefully, she pealed back the layers of my history until I came to understand that I was many things, but not "Normal" in the sense that most people would expect.

[RECORDING]

Following my injuries and debriefing in Viet Nam, I was transferred to the U.S. Navy Hospital at Pearl Harbor on Oahu, HI. With the sudden loss of my father, my mother, Mary Katherine, made her way to Oahu to look after me. As the wife of a recently deceased highly-decorated WWII Navy veteran, she was accorded an amazing amount of courtesy and deference by the hospital command. This literally resulted in her getting a staff room on my floor in the recovery area. Moreover, she was allowed to look in on me at just about any time.

I was healing physically, but mentally and emotionally I was slowly failing. Kate was extremely concerned and could not hide it.

Mary Kate, as was the wont of a woman used to having her way with things took full advantage of the latitude accorded her by the medical staff. As for me, the toll of the events of the fire fight, the death and injuries to the crew with whom I had become so close, and the aftermath of the debriefing, the unwanted praise, and the criticism I feared would be forthcoming, all worked to conspire and deprive me of sleep while raising my anxiety to shocking levels. (I understand all of this better now than I did then, or 4 years later when I was leading up to the Bridge episode.)

My Mom arrived just 2 days after me. I was largely confined to bed - maybe 12-14 hours/day. There were meals, exercise and very limited treatment at the outset. (Please recall that Post Traumatic Stress Disorder (PTSD) was only then beginning to become a condition accorded the medical consensus needed for medical/scientific acceptance and the creation of appropriate courses of treatment.) The biggest problem I was experiencing then was that I felt as if I was functioning in a haze with things around me moving in ever slower motion. Sometimes, I almost felt like my imagination was dictating my experiences. Sometimes, I felt like I could not tell the difference between my fantasies and reality. I know I was given drugs to deal with these "symptoms." What I did not know is whether or not those drugs helped or exacerbated those symptoms. Certainly, the drug they gave me to help me sleep at night intensified some of those feelings. And, of course, I told my mother about this.

We talked multiple times every day. She took at least 2 meals with me every day. She had taken a leave of absence and wanted to see me "get well." For a woman in her early 50s, Mary Catherine looked great. Always busy and diet conscious, she took excellent care of herself. In Oahu, that meant going for walks and sunbathing (not considered unhealthy in those very late 60's – early 70's.). She even had a couple of Bikinis which I teased her about one day and resulted in a good round of laughter and banter. That night it happened for the first time: I dreamed my mother came into my room, took off her robe, wore only undergarments and crawled into my bed next to me. She pulled me against her side and held me. I felt better. She reached down to my crotch and I felt even better. In minutes, I was sound asleep.

This dream, if that's what it was, began to recur nightly. In a few nights, Mom no longer wore undergarments. She had me put my hands on her. She always held me very close. I could smell her at times. She said almost nothing, but when she did, they were endearments. On the last night of these dream-like visits, we had coitus. Her last words, gently said, were, "Thank you, Robert."

Was all of this a dream, imagination, or reality—and could it have been something more complex? My mother never mentioned anything to even suggest that these visits had actually happened, at least as I imagined them. She came in at night to check on me, but was always very quiet so as not to wake me. She never gave a hint to suggest any form of reality to these "symptoms." Since it was my mother, I never thought of telling any doctor about those visits. You are the first one, and only one, to know any of this!

Dr. Arnaud: "Except, perhaps, for your mother."

***

I have NEVER told Mollie or anyone else about this until now. .

36

NEED TO RETHINK
WHERE MY LIFE WAS GOING

After all that had gone on in my life to that Day on the Bridge Rail and the weeks to follow, I was only 30 years old and had just met Margot Arnaud, M.D., Ph.D. of Mill Valley. There was a shift in all of my Bay Area relationships: Sandra was no longer my fiancée nor my friend (enemy?); Carolyn somehow might become a threat if Mollie and I went on with our marriage sooner rather than later; Mollie was a different woman in CA and I was totally taken with her; and then, there was Tinker and his wife, Elaine, Sandra's best friend! WOW!! AND SO, IT CAME TO PASS, in the months ahead that:

I began to see Dr. Arnaud once a week.

Mollie and I became engaged.

Mollie's Dad and my Mom eloped!

I told Carolyn about Mollie.

I did not tell Mollie about Carolyn (but I did tell Dr. Arnaud).

Mollie and I moved in together near the Presidio.

I did not give up my room in Carolyn's apartment.

Elaine forgave me for dumping Sandy.

Sandy married a partner from her father's firm, older and coming off his own nasty divorce I took my first job as a California lawyer with Tinker's firm in Oakland!

Time passed: Mollie and I had our small wedding in San Francisco with a reception in, of course, Philadelphia, a few weeks later. All of the Easterners held out that we would return in a few years. We listened graciously, nodding, but we knew that if our business lives proved successful in California, we were destined to remain there. Our parents seemed to understand this intuitively. Our siblings were a far different story. They thought our new home state was plagued by earthquakes, fires, floods and landslides. Rather than confront their protests head on, we pushed those concerns into the future. (This was a process that I learned from Mollie and Dr. Arnaud. Whereas, I understood the world was not black and white, as did Mollie, so many of our relatives still had vestiges of this ethical imperative. But they could be assuaged by pushing the answer into a non-pressing issue into the future.)

***

(More Summaries of Sessions)

Tinker's law firm was located a block from Jack London Square which is situated on The Oakland Estuary between the mainland and Alameda Island, then home to a huge U.S. Navy Aircraft Carrier Base, which also accommodated multiple aircraft carriers on the north end as well as a large component of support vessels. The Square itself had 4 - 6 restaurants, with more in the vicinity as well as shops and night life. Arriving before 0730, the area across from the office front door was a closing farmers' market which opened about midnight. On 3d Street was the Southern Pacific RR main line between the Mexican and Canadian borders. Two blocks to the west, on the Embarcadero was the Union Pacific main line. (Some of the trains ran to hundreds of cars with multiple engines. Stoppages could shut down the area. Climbing between cars was exceedingly dangerous. Derailments were rare, but always some degree of catastrophic when one occurred.) Offices were sprouting up as older factories were converted and the neighborhood became more gentrified.

A TV Network located a few blocks away (and in the years to come, out of politics, Governor Jerry Brown relocated to a re-built factory, built his own radio broadcast studio as part of his home, went on the air and in a relatively short period relaunched his political career as the two term Mayor of Oakland). The neighborhood was vibrant, adventurous, and a bit dangerous as Oakland had an increasingly elevated crime rate in the '70s, and into the 80's.

Tinker's firm had 3 partners. I was the 4th associate. The firm primarily did civil litigation defense. Most, but not all, came from insurance companies. The partners controlled all of the serious insurance work. Associates assisted, writing motions or responding to them as well as making lesser court appearances. With some training, associates could take or defend depositions, and even prepare "clients" for their depositions. (From the outset, the relationship between the Insurer, its Insured and the attorneys retained by the Insurer to defend the Insured, begged the question of which entity, Insurer or Insured, was the actual "client" of the attorneys in the event of a conflict of interest between those two entities with potentially divergent interests at stake.)

As the most junior associate, I got the unenviable task of doing "subrogation" work. The details are far too dull to recite, but the concepts show some of the powers of the state, here California, and the insurance industry, s/k/a "the Hidden Bankers" (see AIG in the Bush II financial market collapse). My job was to recover the sums paid to an insured by its carrier for that carrier when the other party to the accident was not insured. Then, and now, it is illegal to operate a vehicle in CA without suitable insurance (called "financial responsibility limits"). That uninsured driver cannot defend himself in court (power of both the state and insurance industry) and, if prosecuted, that driver must forfeit his license (same power!). My job was to prosecute these people and use their forfeited license as leverage to collect the sums paid by the Insurer. (The firm got its expenses and one third of the net collections.)

Still, their caseload was increasing and they were very willing to expose me to the various components of civil litigation in the Alameda County Superior and Municipal Courts. Very quickly, I was to find out that each county had its own local rules and this was even true of some individual judges. Within 6 months, I had my first evaluation. Some faults were found, but I was generally congratulated and was given a 20 per cent raise. When I told Mollie that night, she was ecstatic. When I told Dr. Arnaud, she was concerned. She asked me point blank: when was I going to tell Mollie about Carolyn. (I hedged, but thought: NEVER!)

37

CAROLYN IN AN UPWARD SPIRAL

While I was going to law school and getting my life generally in order (after my personal chaos largely brought about by Sandra and her family), Carolyn's career continued to prosper. After the Day on the Bridge, I rarely got back to the Cote d'Azur when Carolyn was present. When I did, Carolyn was gone as her absences had increased in frequency, and then duration, over the years. I began to move my things out and began to leave her notes explaining, not necessarily fully, what had happened. She left me notes as well. Sometimes I left a second note before she picked up the first one. THEN SHE LEFT ME ONE WITH A FEW DATES WHEN SHE WOULD BE THERE and told me she had a car phone which travelled and left a number. I called, got a recording, left a message and told her we needed to talk and when I would be there. A few weeks before the wedding, I arrived and found a Porsche in Carolyn's space. It was a deep copper- a beautiful car. The sun was out and it was a warm day.

Inside, I did not see Carolyn at first. She was on the deck in white shorts and a burgundy top. As she turned slowly to face me, the wind took her hair and blew it gently. She was still the image of the All-American girl — tan, dirty blonde hair, toned body, not voluptuous but healthy-AND that same gorgeous face!

As she stepped into the living room, "So, what have you been up to? An old girl friend from college days and suddenly, you are marrying someone completely different from your Ms. Debutante, and not even from the City?"

She moved toward me, reached out and grabbed me and with no resistance from me, dragged me into her arms. A hug was followed by a warm deep kiss, then another hug, ending with being pushed out to arms' length. "So, please sit. As you said and I shall echo, we really do need to talk. Do you mind if I go first?"

A bit flummoxed, I nodded affirmatively. The next minutes are engraved forever on the back of my brain. Carolyn pulled up a hassock so she would be right in front of me, seemingly a foot away. "His name is Patrick. He has my last name. You are listed on his birth certificate as the father. Do you want a copy?"

I moved from flummoxed to flabbergasted, nodding negatively, as she went on, "You've been busy. You failed to notice when I got a bit bigger, then I was gone, and he was born in New York. My very best girlfriend Violet lives there and she is like his second mother. He is 14 months old. I love him. Do you want Mollie to know?"

Everything I had come to discuss with Carolyn, my whole agenda, had vanished from my thought process in a space of seconds. I tried to get some mental traction. I uttered, "How do you ..."

She filled my pause with the words I knew might come when I paused, "You know that you are the only man I ever cared about sexually. That was true almost 4 years ago when I first told you that very first night and it is still true today. No one else has had the chance to impregnate me. All of my other partners have been women. Violet in New York is the closest I have to a wife. But you know me, sexual fidelity with other women is not a strength for me. So, it was you. And now, here's a picture from last week. Look at those eyes and that brow. He's definitely an O'Neill."

Me, "So, what comes next?"

"Well, if you tell Mollie, or if you want custody, there may be extended negotiations. But if you are reasonable, I am prepared to be reasonable, very reasonable! I want Patrick. Part of you will always be with part of me. I am fascinated by that! If you are in NYC, or he visits here when he's older, he can meet you as an uncle. Someday, he may learn the truth. But that day may be far away, if ever.

"You may worry about supporting him. Don't! I have a trust set up for him. It already has more than $1million. I plan to add to it. The money I am making now is crazy. The trust saves on taxes. This place is now my western office. You can even leave things here. Here's a document cancelling your co-tenancy. Sign it when you're ready. Pay no more. You were there for me when I needed it. The locks will remain unchanged. I will always be there for you in my own way. What do you say?"

"Can I think about it?" my response.

Carolyn, "Yes, but I need to know before you leave here today. I cannot take any chances on your coming up with an alternate plan or doing some crazy thing that will cause me to lose Patrick."

I bowed my head. I needed to think. So many "what ifs" were flashing through my mind. Then I felt her hand on mine, pulling gently, lifting slowly, steering me to her bedroom. In the hour that followed, I decided about the time she put a condom on me (our first).

As I left, she handed me an envelope with Violet's contact info, Patrick's birth certificate, and a signed copy of my cancellation of our joint lease, saying, "I love you and I always will. I am a bit famous and may become more so. I may have to marry someday. I hope not. Most of all, you know how to reach me. Tell Mollie nothing. If she really does not know about me, I suggest you keep it that way, at least for now and the immediate future. If she finds out, I worry that things could be so very different for you, me, and especially Patrick. I do not want that. Let's stay in touch and each have a great life!"

[A note to departed Dr. Arnaud: Hopefully you can read this.

You have no notes about Patrick and I never told anyone until his mother said it was OK to do so and that was after you were gone. Bless you! Ronan.]

38

NOT A REAL HERO

What happened after Viet Nam got me to The Bay Area. This alone, together with the people I knew before I arrived, and those that changed so much while I was absent altered the course of the rest of my life. And, upon sober reflection, I have come to realize that the image the Coast Guard tried to create of me, and for me, as well as my trying to live up to that image may have had a major effect on the person I was to become as a husband, father, lawyer, and yes, as a Coast Guard Reservist. But first and foremost, that image had too much to do with me being on the rail that day.

While in law school, the USCG Reserve people in the 12th Coast Guard District tried to recruit me to become active in the Reserves. I agreed, got my hair cut, uniform clean and shoes polished. I spent one weekend for 12 months, and a 2 week tour of duty, trying to recruit civilians or people with some type of private or public first response or service training into joining the Reserves. Various people tried to train me for this task. The Unit CO wanted to seriously publicize that I was a war hero. As I had a great deal of trouble seeing myself in any role other than that of being fortunate enough to survive that North Viet Nam attack, I was deeply troubled with this as a concept. (When I was transferred back to USCG HQ in DC, my arrival was celebrated as an event, including speeches. Everyone treated me as though I had done something extraordinary. The fuss caused me some emotional trauma. Fortunately, I began to get assigned a lot of special duty. The associated travels often helped, but the ribbon on my chest saying Silver Star never went away. The result: I was almost always treated as someone special.) All during that year, the Viet Nam War continued: singularly unpopular and polarizing in the San Francisco Bay Area! My attempts as a recruiter were an inglorious failure. War heroes were not honored at that time, and especially in that place.

When things closed in on me after law school, now I feel I may have felt subconsciously that I had let not only myself, but so many others, down and that I had betrayed an image they had formed of me. But when I decided to give the Reserves another try, once I had started practicing law, I was assigned to do Legal Assistance. One of the duty stations to which I was assigned was USCG Air Station San Francisco, then a tenant at San Francisco International Airport (SFO) once/quarter. My second trip there, I ran into a helicopter pilot who was an Ensign. We had been in high school together. He had learned to fly as a warrant officer in the Army in Nam. He transferred to USCG, got a commission and this was his first assignment. He saw "the ribbon" and congratulated me on it. He asked what I'd done, so I gave him my self-deprecating answer. He then asked if we could speak frankly. I thought it was about why he was there. He said, in effect, "You don't get that medal unless you saved lives, killed the enemy and do what those around you saw as brave behavior. You may have been afraid, maybe you were even lucky, but you did what you did and others saw you as brave. You owe it to all of them to honor that commendation. That's not just my speech. A Navy LT gave it to me when I was trying to be too humble about my commendations. It's OK to be humble. Just don't forget to be proud of yourself, your comrades, and the service, especially those who gave their lives to it."

Then, he asked me about a divorce, I gave him some advice, and he disappeared never to be seen again. I spent 25 years in the USCG Reserves, functioning mostly as a lawyer. More later, maybe.

39

MORE ABOUT MOLLIE

The Mollie who talked me off the ledge, so to speak, was very different from the Mollie I left behind 6 years before and whom I saw only a few times as those years passed. Not only did she take control of me and the mess I was making of my life, but she somehow seamlessly shifted her career with IBM from the NYC/PHILLY venue, then proceeded to pick up new clients and client applications as if they were low-hanging fruit that had simply been waiting for her to show up. Before long, she was an IBM sales manager in San Francisco.

Her career began changing: first, the mother company entered into yet another consent judgment with the Justice Department (something about domination of the computer marketing by tying programs for client applications to the continued rental of IBM's equipment), which caused them to sell equipment and to give up the source coding to their Disk Operating System to encourage competition (in a few years, HP, Dell, Microsoft and Apple began to fill the void); second, the new IBM business model caused her sales began to drop; and third, Mollie, besides being married, decided she wanted a family while she was still young enough to enjoy the children and still maintain her career.

So, as I was beginning my law career, and became active in the USCG Reserve along with Tinker, we began to engage in love-making without any attempt to forestall the natural results. In a matter of months Mollie was with child and I began a whole new appreciation for my life, our life together and what would be happening in the years ahead.

My Mom was overjoyed as was Mollie's father. But a bit of a

cloud was on the horizon as Mollie's Dad's health began to fade. He was a smoker, and like her mother, had coughed for years. Then, matters became worse: the cough began to produce copious sputum, analysis disclosed potential cancer. Mollie flew home. My Mom sought to help. Mollie's father was on the verge of a breakdown. So was Mollie. She was crying on the telephone every night. The tests were all unclear on whether or not radiation, chemical intervention or surgery were needed. With my Mother's assurance that she would be there for Mollie's father every step of the way and would stay in close touch, Mollie flew home.

I met her at the airport, SFO. She was exhausted to the point of looking haggard. I asked if she was OK?

Mollie, "I think I've been bleeding. I hope I'm not having a miscarriage." Instead of going straight home, we went to the Emergency Room at California Pacific Medical Center {CPMC). The staff swept her into its care and in a matter of minutes, they stabilized the bleeding, got control of her blood pressure, and had her feeling much better in a few hours. Between the rest and positive assessment, Mollie felt relieved. She wanted to go home. So, we did. On the way she mentioned that the OB/GYN had suggested no vaginal sex for a few weeks, until he saw her again. But, back at our apartment, Mollie said, "I want some sex now and I want to bring our baby home to our own house."

I was a bit nonplussed. She pushed me on our bed and began undoing my pants, stopping when she had my belt off, long enough to say, "How about Mill Valley in Marin?"

I briefly thought of the proximity to Carolyn, but then Mollie began to display oral skills I had no idea she possessed.

***

Mollie's Dad had chemotherapy and radiation. He lost his hair. He lost weight. Kate was there the whole time. She brought him home. No one smoked in their house (or ours). Slowly, he gained strength and weight. He went back to work. He came to San Francisco for the Christening of Meaghan Marie. We put them up at the Marines Memorial Club where I was a member. He came to the next christening as well. When his time came, he went with dignity. Kate was tired. She came to see her grand-children twice a year. In a couple of years, we realized she was becoming more alone in Philadelphia as she lost friends and siblings who moved for warmer weather or died. Ultimately, Kate moved to Corte Madera, a few miles from Mill Valley, took up golf and became a women's member at the Peacock Gap Golf Course on the San Rafael peninsula where she made friends and started her whole new life in her mid-60's.

40

CRITICAL SESSION

*O*f all the times Dr. Arnaud and I met, there were some sessions that meant more to my moving forward with my life
than others. After months of sessions, there came a time when
fixing the reasons for the Bridge Incident became critical.

We had fixed on Sandra, the job at her father's firm, my Viet
Nam issues, the bizarre dreamlike recollections about my Mom,
even my relationships with Mollie and Carolyn. We quickly dis-
posed of Mollie as not in my mind at the time; then Carolyn,
who was a casual concern but not a source of issues then. The
war, my injuries and my time in Pearl Harbor were a different
story. I felt their combined effect caused an internal change in
my emotional make-up, which then impacted my thought
processes. Then, together with the alcohol and Cannabis, I had
become less certain in my decisions and had an increasing sense
of diminished self-worth. Yet, I had left the East, relocated, accomplished law school and had undertaken the beginning of a
career. Much of my life had proven uncertain. This left me confused.

But I kept coming back to Sandra as the root cause of that
day's behavior. From the beginning of our relationship, Sandra
had made it clear, more impliedly than expressly, that I was
moving into an arena that was above my former station in life.
Moreover, her family, and especially her parents acted and
spoke as if this elevation in my status was an absolute truth.
Whatever I did, achieved, said, or stood for was always
markedly below the standards at which the Allens lived their
lives. Sandra had an air of entitlement. She was truly beautiful,

exceptionally intelligent, and poised. Her voice rarely raised. She spoke with a seemingly perfect modulation. Yet, I wondered if she was at all happy, even when she told me that she loved me. Sometimes, I self-espoused the concept that her parents had somehow offended her, and by marrying me, she would achieve something beyond their control. She would ignore or make light of these kind of remarks.

Then there was the sex issue with Sandra. Following my first oral sex with her, her requests slowly increased until I was feeling unfulfilled every time we got together. Also, I began to wonder if this phase of our Life was an indicator of a potential pervasively increasing selfish behavior to follow.

Finally, there was Sandra's attitude toward the job. She talked about the firm incessantly, including her assignments, the politics and the jockeying for positions within the firm. The more I listened, the more I became uncertain and confused about my ability to fit in both on a legal intellectual level as well as dealing with the politics, especially once "I was married to the boss's daughter." (This proved especially confusing because at times when I initiated discussions on the Firm, she would tell me they were inappropriate in some form or another.)

Mr. Allen did nothing to ameliorate these misgivings and made it equally apparent that issues like these concerning the firm and my role in it were not to be discussed by him at his level, that of managing partner. When I made my declaration to Sandy about not working at the firm, I think I was really looking for her to explain to me why I was wrong and everything would turn out to be alright. Instead, within the space of a few minutes, 3 years of planning evaporated in the maelstrom of her uncontrolled anger, and I was suddenly feeling more than a bit dispossessed and despondent. A few too many drinks, and Voila!! Thus, with my disassociation from the firm, followed by my complete break-up with Sandra, viewed from my current perspective and with more than sufficient analysis to assess these options, I finally came to a clearer appreciation of the main reason why I drove myself to act as I did on the Bridge. Of course, there were latent others!

Fixing myself came next.

41

A TURNING POINT OR TWO

When Mollie announced that she was pregnant, I came to realize that one of my great life-changing events was about to occur. Yes, I was already a father, but those circumstances were completely foreign to being told that my wife was going to give birth in seven months. Carolyn's child was a story, this was the real thing! My career was beginning to take-off, but I did not feel it was airborne. As Mollie glowed and we hugged, I realized she was the primary wage earner. It did not begin to occur to me at that moment that Mollie would want to continue her career.

In our years together, I had come to appreciate how smart, energetic and detailed my wife was in living her life. Still, there were just the two of us. Our apartment in Mill Valley might not be big enough, or suitable, for a child. How would we handle all the changes and the new needs?

Of course, most of my concerns had already occurred to Mollie. In the days to come, she surprised me with her answers: she would continue her career with IBM, we would have a nanny, and we would buy a bigger house right away. With both of us working, we could afford all of this. Pay raises would allow us to save. It was a time to be happy, not to worry.

Busy as she was, all of these events came to pass and more. The months flew by. The putative grandparents appeared at different times to pledge their support. We took Lamaze classes and bought baby furniture. There were showers. We moved and decorated. All was in readiness.

6.5 months later at 2 a.m., Mollie woke me. We drove to

Marin General Hospital. I called my office at 7 a.m. to tell them I would not be in and to ask that they cover my calendar. After 12 hours of labor, the OB/GYN was concerned that Mollie was not dilating properly and a vaginal birth might prove dangerous for mother and child. Mollie tried a spinal injection to assist the dilation by relaxing her, but it had little or no effect. At that point I urged her to undergo a Caesarian as the doctor recommended. As committed as she was to "natural childbirth," Mollie relented and agreed. Maeve Marie came into our lives. 3 days later we went home as a family. The Christening was a major event.

Robert Emmett was born 2 years later. Mollie began to look for a bigger house in a warmer section of Mill Valley. I was named Executive Officer of a Coast Guard Reserve unit at USCG Base Alameda. Only one other reserve lawyer was left to carry on legal assistance. That was a concern, but that mission would be among my responsibilities as XO.

On 1 JAN 1980, I became a partner at the law firm.

Becoming a father and having some successes began to have a positive impact on my uncertain evaluations of my self-worth. But at least once every month, I still went to see Dr. Arnaud. Mollie and I never discussed those visits.

42

KLEIN KELLY & WEINBERG, PLLC

My time at Tinker's firm began to move quickly. One day my workload was mostly subrogation; then, to get more court time on my feet, there was some domestic relations work, which began to grow at an exponential rate; and then, came the cases where I became the lead attorney with diminishing partner supervision in certain matters. This progression in a law career, as it turns out, was out of the ordinary for the path to partner. And, I was at this point, less than 2 years into practice when Jerry Klein called me into his corner office and said,

"Our biggest insurance client asked if we could do an Admiralty case? Sean Kelly told them we have 2 Coast Guard officers as associates and he came to see me. Tinker has absolutely no Admiralty experience. How about you?"

Me, "I sat in on a few sessions at Hastings. It is a bit of its own world, but the case itself may be more fact dependent. We may be able to get through it without any indication it's a first case for the office."

Jerry looked at me over the top rims of his spectacles, "This is a very important client. We've had 5 auto PI cases to defend from them. This represents a major jump."

My concern was his concerns and I needed to know more about the nature of the case. So, "Jerry, if you tell me something about it, maybe I can relieve your concerns a bit."

He paused, picked up what looked like a pleading and handed it to me. I read the first 10 or 12 pages, enough to get the basic facts of the case: a sailboat explosion, a fire, injuries, but no deaths. It took place *off* the CA coast just south of Point Arguello. I thought for a few seconds and said, "Must have been a motor- sailor from the description of the incident. The time of day indicates that the crew failed to clear the fuel fumes from the bilges before hitting the engine starter. Result: fire ball!"

Jerry said, "We cannot spare Tinker to work on this. You go it alone and report to me. Have you done an initial evaluation letter yet?" I nodded affirmatively. He added, "Please try to have a draft of this one to me in a few days."

My first lead counsel case!

***

This case allowed me to begin to set myself apart from the other attorneys in the firm.

KKW was what was shortly to become known in the legal industry as an Insurance Defense firm. Not a bad thing, but a label that would lead insurance companies to see the work that these firms undertook as somewhat repetitious, and in the end, fungible. A development that would later play a role in facilitating a major role change in my life.

***

The key turning point in the Point Arguello case came about at a fairly early stage. Trans California Insurance Company had retained KKW to represent its insured, the Oxnard Marina, the last point of service for the *Rum Runner*, an 86 foot ketch rigged motor schooner. The ship's owner filed a motion in federal court for limitation of liability. Some Admiralty research by me indicated that if an owner was not on board a ship involved in an actionable event, then the maximum value recoverable for that event was limited to the value of the ship itself in its damaged condition (not so good if the ship sank). The motion claimed that the owner was not on board, but the owner was a trust. The Declaration of a putative trustee asserted that no trustee was on board. Therefore, no owner. (Now, the ship's attorneys were an old San Francisco Admiralty firm. It would seem they should be trustworthy.) Rather than respond to the motion itself, I brought a Cross Motion to Strike the Supporting Declaration on the grounds of Hearsay and The Best Evidence Rule. I also asked that the cross-motion be decided first as it deprived my client of an opportunity to adequately oppose the Ship Owner's Motion since the Trust document itself was not attached to the motion anywhere..

The Court basically agreed with us. A second Declaration was forthcoming with a copy of the trust attached. The trust was revocable during the lifetime of the trustor who was Fred Arnesen. Mr. Arnesen was sleeping in the owner's cabin when the fuel supply blew up. He received a broken arm and minor bums. He swore he was not a trustee. However, since the trust was revocable at Arnesen's sole discretion, we argued he should be deemed the owner on board by the Court. The Motion to Limit Liability was DENIED.

We brought in 2 experts: one on salvage to explain the damages and the other, a retired Coast Guard Chief Boatswain's Mate, to explain the most likely cause of the incident. Ultimately, but at the first opportunity, we settled for an extremely nominal amount. Jerry Klein and I were invited to TCIC's home office where we were greeted by the maritime claims manager and the company's VP of Claims. We met much of their claims staff following lunch in their cafeteria. At the end of a short day, the VP of Claims and the maritime manager asked to take us for a drink. At the ensuing meeting, we were asked to be available as a resource to the company for all of its maritime claims as our office was especially well suited to this role. After a brief discussion of fees, we agreed and departed shortly thereafter.

Now, I was a hero at the firm. So was Tinker who had

brought me in. Our workload from TCIC took off. A few days before Christmas, right before the firm party, the 3 partners were gathered in Jerry Klein's office. When they called Tinker and me in, I was still in my 30's and had been with the firm a touch under 3 years. Tinker was there for a bit more than 4. They offered us partnerships: We were on our way!!

43

CAREER CHANGERS:
"DUKES OF HAZARD"

As a young partner, I began to get my own cases. I had come to know the local claims professionals at a number of insurance companies that were clients of the firm. A number of them insured trucking companies. One referred a case involving two deaths and two serious injury matters. One of our senior partners took the case, but before he could write the initial report to the company, he was involved in a serious accident himself. As the others were busy and I had done work for the carrier that case made its way to me.

Four young men, ages 16 and 17, were out joy riding in a convertible sedan owned by one of the 17 year old driver's parents. They all had consumed a few beers, but none had a blood alcohol over 0.10. (Then, the CA threshold for Driving While Under the Influence of Alcohol [DWI].) The top was down and they were doing some tricks and some speeding, according to friends and one witness. They saw an elevated train track ahead. The driver gunned the car and took the up ramp at an estimated speed of 67 MPH. Although unclear precisely how high, or how far, the convertible went airborne, the car could not steer in the air. When it landed on the other side of the track, it travelled about 50 feet when the right side of the convertible went under the left rear of our client's stake body truck. Both of those boys sitting on the right met gruesome deaths. The sudden deceleration and lack of restraints caused the other two to suffer multiple fractures and a variety of soft tissue injuries. One lawyer represented all 4 sets of interests in that one law suit. Our client, The Trucker, was the only defendant. Their case was based on our client's failure to have underride protection on the rear comers of the truck and that it was parked too close to the tracks so as to constitute a hazard.

After consulting a couple of my partners, including Tinker, I suggested to the carrier that we answer the complaint and cross-complain against the driver, his parents, and the parents of the other occupants as well. That procedural legal issue was problematic then in CA because a defendant was not permitted to add new parties to an existing lawsuit under CA law. Still, I made a case for changing the law to the carrier, essentially saying this was a case that would support a change in the law on appeal. To my surprise, and that of my partners, the carrier agreed. (Although insurance carriers are inherently conservative and were reluctant to expand liability, insurers for truckers were too often perceived as deep pockets and needed to spread the risk as well as gain leverage to facilitate settlements.)

Our motion to file the Cross-Complaint on behalf of the Trucker was denied at the trial court level. We proceeded to seek a Writ of Mandamus to the trial court from the Court of Appeals by telling the trial court that it was changing the law as a deprivation of the Trucker's due process rights relative to those suing him. Instead of the usual summary denial, we received notice from that appellate court that our petition was under advisement. No one in the office was quite sure what that meant, but we advised the carrier that this novel procedural step might turn out to be positive.

When the attorney for the plaintiff interests sought to move the case forward, we moved the trial court to stay the matter pending a decision by the appellate court. The trial court ordered a 30 day stay. Before that time was up, the California Supreme Court published its opinion in *Li v. Yellow Cab* allowing a defendant to name new defendants in a Cross Complaint. That case involved an alleged failure of parental supervision as did our case. The Trucker client was ecstatic, and his insurance carrier was most pleased.

A lengthy series of motions ensued in the trial court. Each of the plaintiff interests suddenly had to employ its own counsel and the original plaintiffs' attorney for all was barred as conflicted for representing interests that were now suing each other. At a lengthy settlement conference, the Trucker's liability insurer settled all four sets of plaintiff interests for less than $100,000. Considering the risks attendant with two deaths and two exceedingly serious injury matters, that carrier was incredibly pleased and I began to get my own cases from them, as well as an invitation to meet some of their senior claims staff in Scottsdale: a carrier called Desert Mutual.

My partners were pleased and our workload began to increase markedly.

44

DESERT MUTUAL

D esert Mutual was exactly what its name implies: a mutual insurance company owned by its members, founded in Phoenix during the Great Depression to insure those doing business in the greater Phoenix area. Over time, its business and its membership grew throughout Arizona. As some of its members became larger and opened places of business in California, Nevada, New Mexico, Colorado, Utah and beyond, the mutual became licensed to practice in more than 30 states by the time I went to visit their home office in Scottsdale, just off the boulevard of the same name in McCormick Ranch.

During that half century of growth, Desert Mutual had become a broader based carrier undertaking a variety of personal lines of coverage as well as trucking and other commercial enterprises. In all, it was viewed in the insurance industry as a casualty carrier whose primary contracts were to defend and indemnify its insureds/members.

My first visit to Desert Mutual's Headquarters was in the Spring of 1983 and it was close to 100 degrees. I parked, found the front desk, registered and got my visitor's badge. I was scheduled to see the claims staff. A gentleman named Larry Decker met me in reception, loudly saying, "Ronan, Am I happy to meet you! That was one great piece of lawyering you pulled off for us! Follow me."

With that, I fell in behind Larry, whose name I recognized from being the signatory on various company documents. He whisked me through doorways and corridors (many office buildings in Greater Phoenix are only one or two floors and tend to sprawl). Eventually, we came to the Executive Suite. Larry went to a door that said, Chester Moeller, entered, and was introduced to the VP of Claims who rose and escorted us into the conference room. There I actually met Manny Garcia, Major Claims, for whom I had worked on the "Dukes Case" as we began to refer to it. Also, I shook hands with Gerry Dwyer, in charge of Casualty.

Chester got right to the point. Several years back, a company called Wallboard had its primary coverage of $1,000,000 for BI and PD with SF Casualty, a major carrier headquartered near San Francisco. They had been the primary Comprehensive General Liability carrier (CGL in that business; now called Corporate in lieu of Comprehensive). Wallboard made a variety of building materials which contained asbestos as a component. In the last few years leading up to the Desert Mutual event, the amount of asbestosis Bodily Injury cases had increased markedly when, out of the blue, SF Casualty gave notice to Wallboard that it would be dropping Wallboard as a primary insured in 30 days.

Chester Moeller paused, perhaps for emphasis, then said, "Millard Granger, then the Risk Manager for Wallboard, and I go back many years, decades. His brokers could not get any of the usual primary CGL carriers to even speak with him. He called me and asked if we would underwrite his primary policy for the balance of that year to support his excess coverages while he tried to find some other entity to act as a primary. Also, he offered to exclude all asbestos claims."

He went on to explain that DMIC had no one to write an exclusion as they used forms from the Insurance Services Office (ISO) which specialized in writing coverages, including CGLs. With that Millard agreed to write the exclusion. Chester took it to Underwriting and Marketing, and for a hefty premium, DMIC agreed to cover Wallboard for those few months. When they could not get coverage by the policy expiration date, we agreed renew for another year at the full hefty premium.

Toward the end of that second year, they got a new primary carrier and Millard left for a better job in the Midwest.

Being a bit naive, I asked what about the exclusion. They answered that not all asbestos BI cases have turned out to be for Asbestosis, the operative *exclusionary* word used in the exclusion. Some were for lung cancer and other types of cancer. But the plaintiffs all claimed asbestos exposure as the cause of each disease process. I asked about Mr. Granger's current location. He went with a giant retail enterprise headquartered in Cincinnati as its Risk Manager and Director of Claims. Chet Moeller thought Granger would be cooperative.

They wanted a total defense and to get out as early as possible. They wanted someone creative to lead the defense. They wanted me.

I asked to include Tinker and explained our arrangement. They told me the suggested fee (far above anything I was aware of the firm charging). I asked to be excused for a few minutes and called the office. Klein got Kelly on the line. When I told them the stakes and the fees, I sensed the mute button go on by virtue of a complete silence. Klein came back on, "We think one of us should be the lead counsel on something this big."

I explained they wanted me (with Tinker) and why. I stressed the need to act promptly as the time to plead was running AND that was why I called. AND the Desert Mutual people were waiting at the table. The name partners began to get the picture. A brief pause, again on mute, and then, "Go ahead, but you need to keep us informed."

The deal was done on a handshake. Manny and Gerry would be my day-to-day contacts, with Larry Decker responsible. Chet Moeller was recusing himself from everything to do with the matter as he was a potential witness.

45

LUNCH IN PHOENIX

Dudley excused himself from lunch, but said he would join us the next time I was in town. The visitor parking spaces were closer, so I drove. The Biltmore Hotel, as Gerry recited, was a Frank Lloyd Wright project. It was low, grey stone and exuded gravitas. The dining room was mostly outdoor and was much more desert casual then the somewhat stern lobby and its restaurant. We were given a table with a degree of privacy. Larry sat across from me; Manny and Gerry on either side. Little did I suspect at that moment that some of this group and I would work together for almost 15 years; or that its dissolution would be life changing for me and many others.

No one ordered any type of alcoholic beverage: 3 iced teas and I had ginger ale. We ordered quickly. Then Larry began to get into the details of the circumstances surrounding Wallboard, Inc. and the building materials manufacturers in the U.S.A. (These products have relatively low $ value compared to their weight, so transportation costs mandate that these companies either have many plants or are more regional in nature.) The problem was asbestos, a mineral that had fire retardant qualities, when inhaled in sufficient quantities could break down the body's immune system and turn it against itself by creating scarring in the lung which grew on itself much like a form of cancer. That disease was called asbestosis.

Desert Mutual had written that one partial year of coverage and a few more months of a second year, a few years before. The only disease discussed at that time of the negotiations with the Wallboard risk manager was asbestosis. Since then, lawsuits for lung cancer and some other pulmonary condition called mesothelioma were being filed. The Desert Mutual policy's exclusion for asbestos, as drafted, actually used the word "asbestosis" rather than a phrase like "caused by asbestos" creating a potentially more limited term to define the claims which desert Mutual would not cover by virtue of this agreed exclusion. No one knowing any better, and relying on the Wallboard risk manager known by several of the insurer's people as a straight shooter, Desert Mutual went ahead and accepted the wording in the exclusion and issued its manuscript policy. Now, with that risk manager gone, lawsuits claiming a disease other than asbestosis were being tendered to Desert Mutual by the San Francisco attorneys for Wallboard.

Meanwhile, San Francisco Casualty, the predecessor insurer to Desert Mutual had sued Wallboard claiming it did not owe a defense or any indemnity for claims made for diseases which were not discovered during the many years that the SFC's primary policies covered Wallboard. (This was a "trigger of coverage" theory called" Manifestation." The other pending theory being advanced by some insureds was that the claimant need only be exposed to its products during those years of coverage to trigger SFC's obligations; hence, the "Exposure" trigger of coverage.)

What Desert Mutual wanted was to get out of this coverage morass as soon as practicable. They had tried negotiating with no success. Their usual CA counsel, which had excess carriers as clients in this litigation, was considered too prestigious for this matter. So, there I sat. What to do? Rather than start that and with the time given to this input briefing at lunch, it was time to go. As Larry took the check, he said, "You will be reporting to me, but be sure that Manny and Gerry are copied on everything. This is a very serious matter as the number of claims might prove open ended. We will stay in contact with each other so whomsoever contacts you will speak for all of us (he actually used "whomsoever" in a sentence. I remember it to this day!)."

In the rental car, Larry handed me a package as they all exited. We shook hands all round. Everyone's grip was firm, especially Gerry's.

The letter retaining our firm and me was explicit, yet open-ended, on means to attain the goal. The rate Desert Mutual would pay was $25/hour more than our highest usual rate. My partners were pleased, but time changes most relationships.

46

LIFE MOVES ON

By 1984, I was fully committed time-wise between all of my cases, the Coast Guard Reserve duty which took up 12 weekends and 2 weeks, and my life at home with 2 children and a very interesting, entertaining wife. Then things started to change!

Elaine, Tinker's wife and mother of their only child, Bonita, was asked by her growing firm to relocate to Washington, D.C. to open an office. They asked Tinker to join her while he sought a new firm. They offered fantastic money. Reluctantly, Tinker gave notice to his partners that he was going to leave. He told me, and Desert Mutual agreed, that he could continue to work on the Wallboard Coverage matter.

Tinker found a new firm in D.C. It had offices only in D.C. and New York. He was going to do environmental coverage work. Desert Mutual approved him continuing on the Wallboard matter. Because his firm charged a higher rate, Tinker would cost more than me. So, Desert Mutual set up a special rate structure for the defense of its coverage cases and began to pay me and our associates at the same rate as Tinker and his people. The other partners were not happy about this ...a first real sign of forthcoming discontent.

Meanwhile, at about this same time, who should reappear? Carolyn! One day she just called my office and asked to see me for lunch. We met at a small, very upscale seafood restaurant on the Sausalito waterfront. It seemed like it had been years. She was the same, but somehow different; smoother, more assured-which was saying something because Carolyn never lacked self-confidence. After almost an hour of catching up, she produced a small handful of photographs — they all showed Patrick who looked like a male version of Carolyn at a distance, but quite like me in close-ups. "Do you want these?" she asked.

I thought for a minute or two and then said, "Yes." My life would never be quite the same again.

"I told Patrick I have some good friends in California and that one of them is like a big brother to me. That would be you, Uncle Ronan. That's how he knows you. What I do need are photos of you? They could even include some of your children and Mollie. Will you send them?" And that was it. Patrick would be in my life going forward. So would Carolyn.

As we sipped our coffee, Carolyn looked over the rim of her cup, mischief in her eyes, "Can you spare an hour back at our place?" It was more like 2 hours. I had called the office and told them I had an upset stomach from lunch.

47

WALLBOARD MANUEVERING

Months began to slip by as motions were filed in the SFC/Wallboard case. The court in San Francisco finally appointed a single judge to deal with the Wallboard case which came to have more than 20 parties between primary and excess insurers, many of which had multiple years of coverage. San Francisco Casualty (SFC) had initiated the suit, but Wallboard's attorneys brought in virtually all of the insurer parties by Cross-Complaint, including Desert Mutual. SFC amended its Complaint to name all of Wallboard's insures including our client. With approval from Phoenix, we filed an Answer to both the Complaint and the Cross Complaint denying any duties to Wallboard on behalf of Desert Mutual, affirmatively alleging its Asbestos Exclusion, and in filing a Cross-Complaint seeking a declaratory judgment against all parties as to Desert Mutual's duties and obligations as well as costs of suit from Wallboard and SFC.

When the case seemed ready to progress to Discovery (a process to secure documents and witness testimony), a judicial panel ordered that 3 other cases involving similar issues be joined with the Wallboard matter to provide a single, consistent resolution and process for essentially the same issues. The judge assigned to Wallboard recused himself at the outset because of a claim of potential bias by one of the primary carriers involved in 3 of the 4 cases (Desert Mutual was only in one case: Wallboard). The panel appointed another judge whose first step was to ask for briefs from each party on the process they felt would lead to a fair and efficient outcome.

Since the various parties had different objectives and timing goals, they were at serious variance. For example, all of the manufacturers wanted to have as many years of coverage as possible and a trigger of coverage that would maximize their defense and indemnity benefits.

Most of the primary carriers wanted a trigger of coverage for the year of first disease manifestation only and they wanted their duty to defend to end when their policy limits were exhausted. The excess carriers wanted to drag the matter out for as long as possible, to pay no defense costs, and to have all primary and excess coverage below their level exhaust before *they* paid dollar one. All of the briefs were lengthy, some running to more than a box of documents with exhibits. Time seemed to work against the manufacturers whose primary policies for some years might exhaust.

The second judge held his first hearing on all of those briefs almost 4 months to the day that the first San Francisco Superior Court Judge recused himself. At the outset, Judge Williams announced that he had a prepared filing to read into the case record. Succinctly, his wife had a trust fund which held stock in 5 of the parties to the litigation. As such, he felt an absolute necessity that he recuse himself for a conflict of interest. The air seemed to go out of the room.

Seven days later, the Judicial Panel announced that the Honorable Isadore Greenberg would preside over the matter. 2 days later, Judge Greenberg announced that he would have a hearing one week hence in the San Francisco Board of Supervisors Chambers and that all parties were to be present and represented by counsel. Party representatives were encouraged to attend, but it was not mandatory.

That hearing was relatively brief. No party sought to recuse the judge. He appointed a former law clerk of his, now a partner in a prestigious firm, to provide a summary of every hearing to every party via counsel. Finally, he required every party to deposit by no later than 60 days every non privileged, arguably relevant document in its possession in a repository to be ascertained in that 60 day interim and to create a Privilege Log for every document sought to be withheld (log details followed). He declined to answer questions. The hearing ended in an uproar. Counsel for Johns Manville could be heard to say they had more than 7,000,000 documents that would need to be reviewed. Many similar sentiments were uttered: few were in praise of the judge.

After spending a few hours thinking about the order and consulting with Tinker, the two of us set up a conference call with Larry, Manny and Gerry in Phoenix. First, we talked about their company's Wallboard documents, including the claims correspondence. They allowed this could be 1,000s of pages. Then, Tinker and I broached the subject of other potentially impacted Desert Mutual insureds which might manufacture or distribute products that contained asbestos. Silence followed at the other end. Were we certain all of this was needed? I explained again about Judge Greenberg (tough and very smart) and I was certain this was included. They said they would start gathering files. They asked me to come down to Phoenix. I acquiesced.

Within 24 hours, they had files on more than 20 of their historical insureds. Some were multiple banker's boxes. Then, Manny said, "Follow me ..." as he led me down a hall to a room. Upon opening the door, I was confronted with stacks of banker's boxes. 20, maybe 30, boxes occupied the center of the room. "These are CAL Board claim files. Do you think we need to produce these?"

At that point, I understood why they wanted me there. Discussions with outside counsel would assure the Attorney-Client privilege applied to the ensuing discussions about all of the non-Wallboard files. I asked to get Tinker on a speaker phone, And the 5 of us settled into the potentially relevant files that would need to be produced AND what to do about withholding the identity of Desert Mutual insureds which were not interested parties in the Wallboard or other cases before Judge Greenberg (other issues were discussed as well, but this meeting set the tenor for the next 15 years of my life.).

We ultimately decided that the documents which were potentially relevant dealt with the overall underwriting history of each insured as well as the initial tender, response and follow-up on all environmental claims submitted by each to Desert Mutual. Also, we decided at the hearing in 3 weeks to seek an order allowing the redaction of the identity of each non-Wallboard insured, substituting a letter code for each (23 of them.). Tinker started right to work on that motion and we filed it under seal before the Court closed the next day.

Three weeks later, I arrived at the court to see that the Desert Mutual motion was second on Judge Greenberg's docket and the matter was again set to be heard in the San Francisco Board of Supervisors Chamber. Judge Greenberg took his bench promptly at 10:00 a.m. His clerk called the first matter, a request for an extension of time for 6 months to comply with the Judge's production order brought by Johns Manville, the lead defendant in all asbestos litigation nationwide, one of the matters joined with Wallboard by the California Judicial Counsel. Judge Greenberg stared out over his glasses at Moses Gibbs, a New York lawyer specially admitted in California to appear in this matter and those directly related to it, and said," Were you here 4 weeks ago, Mr. Gibbs, when I handed down my production order?"

Gibbs answered, "Yes, Your Honor."

"Did you hear me ask if anyone of you had any questions about my very brief order?" the Judge continued.

Gibbs replied, "No, Your Honor."

"There could be no questions at that time , Mr. Gibbs?, because my Order was brief, clear and specific. Am I wrong?"

"No, Your Honor."

"Mr. Gibbs, I gather you have been associated for some period of time with your client on this matter and have appeared across the country on its behalf during that time. Moreover, your reputation proceeds you in my court room today. I have read the details of your motion. I suggest that your client hire a great many more people to start reviewing its documents AND that you get your hands dirty helping out. Your first production is due in 28 days and with it, I want a status report on when it will be complete."

Gibbs, looking smarmy, "Thank you, Your Honor.'

"That's not all, Mr. Gibbs. While all the years have been going past on the underlying litigation, and the coverage issues have mounted, I find it extremely unseemly that no one saw fit to begin a process like this when litigation became more than a mere potential. For that reason and to emphasize my lack of tolerance for your client's general dereliction, I find sanctions of $100,000 appropriate. So ordered. Next!"

I rose, Judge Greenberg looked over his glasses and seemed to grin ever so slightly, and said, "Mr. O'Neill has appeared before me for years now. I suggest that all of you read his client's motion. It is reasonable and I grant it. Mr. O'Neill, you will have the Desert Mutual files on this Wallboard available for production at their home office in Phoenix in 28 days?"

Me, "Yes, Your Honor."

Judge Greenberg, "And how many days will it take you to redact and make available the other 23 Desert Mutual insureds' potentially relevant documents?'

"An additional 28 days," I responded.

"So ordered. Any party wishing to withdraw a motion may do so now. However, I do intend to call the entire docket having read through all of this material."

I stayed for about 5 more motions. Sanctions were a matter of routine. I called Tinker from a pay phone in City Hall and he was able to get Larry and Manny on the phone. All three were shocked by the sanctions, but extremely pleased by our outcome. Forces of Darkness were lurking as I would find out in not many days.

48

A PATH TO VICTORY?

Most of the law firms involved in the coverage cases for their insurance clients or the policyholders were huge. But not all, including ours. With four huge cases consolidated for discovery and trial, staffing often involved sizeable teams. That was something we sought to avoid for Desert Mutual. After all, we had little more than one year of coverage, an arguable asbestos exclusion drafted by Wallboard's former risk manager, and only a few potentially relevant witnesses. Nonetheless, Wallboard's counsel, lead by Sandra's father, wanted to take multiple lines of depositions simultaneously. We opposed this tactic, joined by a number of other smaller firms whose clients had more limited exposure. The Discovery Commissioner ruled in our favor and the Judge backed him.

In response Wallboard's attorneys set depositions every Tuesday through Friday of every week for 44 straight weeks broken only by some holidays. How to get Millard Granger's deposition completed to support a summary judgment motion became the key to success. After consulting with Gerry Dwyer and Manny Garcia, we tried something novel: We noticed the deposition of Former Wallboard Risk Manager Granger for every Monday in Oakland until complete. (To persuade Mr. Ganger to fly to San Francisco or Oakland, Desert Mutual had to agree to pay for 1st class airfare, a nice hotel and the same for Mrs. Granger for an unknown number of weekends.)

Ultimately, in his deposition, Mr. Granger testified that Desert Mutual was willing to underwrite the needed primary coverage to support Wallboard's entire primary property and casualty insurance program while their broker shopped for the next year's coverage. (Without this type of primary coverage, all of the layers of excess and catastrophic coverages above the primary level could never be triggered as Wallboard would be in breach of its coverage obligations to all of its excess carriers.) To get this emergency coverage, Granger not only agreed to an Asbestos Exclusion in that Wallboard primary policy but also he agreed to write an exclusion that would be satisfactory to Wallboard and Desert Mutual, which he did.

When asked if it was meant to exclude only "Asbestosis," as he wrote, he went on to testify that "asbestosis" was intended to exclude any and all claims arising out of any type of Bodily Injury alleged in any manner whatsoever to have been caused in whole or part by exposure to asbestos fibers of any type. (At that point in time, further diseases and their causative relationship to asbestos exposure were less known. Thus, Mr. Granger testified he used that word and further acknowledged that the insurance industry terminology in the ensuing years had evolved to "asbestos related disease" with many varying qualifications.)

I managed to elicit this testimony and Mr. Granger's business background all on the first day of deposition. One of the excess carriers over Desert Mutual then began its cross-examination. Wallboard's attorney, including one day by Sandy Allen (aloof toward me) took 4 days. In all, Mr. Granger testified for 17 days — ALL Mondays, ALL in Oakland.

Gerry Dwyer came up to watch the 3d Monday. She stayed at the Palace Hotel in San Francisco. I got to pick her up and drop her off. She was very impressed with how well Mr. Granger's testimony helped her company and with the novel means of completing his deposition. She was also impressed with the Palace.

She liked it so much, she asked me in for a drink. I accepted.

On the way to the bar, she told me how much she liked her room and asked if I would like to see it. Having never been past the conference room floors, I allowed I would like to see it.

I saw a lot more. BIG mistake!

49

AS TIME MOVED ON

While I was involved in the Wallboard matter, I also became involved with other clients. Some were insurers and some their insureds which began to use us for non-insurance matters. Our firm continued to grow. Tinker and I were a team and we were generating more business and fees than any other team.

Mollie and I were the parents of a boy and a girl. She decided we needed a new home which resulted in a sit down discussion. The issue was put out by her when asking if we should have more children, and if so, how many and when? After some thought with give and take, we decided we would have one more, but buy a place that would hopefully support that one more if that came to pass. We also decided to look further north in Marin County as the commute to Oakland was getting harder every year and the public schools were better for the most part. Mollie took care of the rest.

Another issue mentioned that night was Mollie's career. IBM wanted her to relocate. As a mother of two, she was unable to do that. Her manager, not located locally, essentially told her that if she would not relocate, she would be stuck in her current position and probably "leap-frogged for promotions." Neither of us wanted to believe this was true, but I advised Mollie to make a memo of the discussion. She did.

Mollie found the right house for us in northern Mill Valley, not far from its quaint downtown with cute shops and restaurants. It was more than a bit of a fixer upper and the local property taxes were quite high. Nonetheless, we both saw it as our potential home for the rest of our lives. After getting some major remodeling done with the help of lower interest rates, refinancing more than once and a very friendly bank that also did my firm's banking, Mollie became pregnant with our third. When she returned from her first trip to the OB/GYN, Mollie announced that not only was she pregnant, but she was going to have twins!!

The news of twins sent the whole family, including all of the our siblings, into a state of euphoria. Visions of relatives descending on our house began to frighten us both, but we were steadfast in the face of this potential. The real main issue was Mollie's job. Although she was highly thought of, her boss was unhappy that she would not relocate. Now, with twins on the way, we were concerned how he would react. At first, we were pleasantly surprised by his attitude: positivity bordering on solicitude. But over a few months, it became clear that he was hoping Mollie would not return from maternity leave. This set Mollie on edge.

As the time to give birth drew near, Mollie set up a scheduled last day to work. Her work friends gave her a shower. She continued some tasks at home for clients, but gradually stopped. A few days before the birth, she got a call from a woman who was a recruiter seeking Mollie specifically to go to work for a firm in what the recruiter was calling "Silicon Valley." The recruiter seemed aware that Mollie was pregnant and would be very limited for travel for many months ahead. She said her client was interested in Mollie's ability to create novel and imaginative applications and that she could spend part of each week working from home! The money offered was almost double what Mollie currently made.

After the call, we talked about it. Mollie had a Non-Disclosure Agreement and a Non-Compete Agreement with IBM. Those could make the new job prospect bleak. She called the recruiter back the next day and told her. The woman was not at all concerned. She advised that her client had attorneys who routinely dealt with NDAs and NCAs. The recruiter told Mollie that her client would clear the way for her to accept its offer while she was in recovery. Mollie agreed to that.

Mollie gave birth to a pair of healthy babies- Meaghan Marie and Patrick Michael. June, the recruiter, sent an enormous array of flowers. Robin, Mollie's boss at IBM, sent one also. It included a note which talked about working conditions for Mollie similar to those suggested by June's client. No money was mentioned. A few days went by. Mollie brought the twins home. Robert and Maeve were beside themselves with joy. Mary Katherine was there the next day-fussing and working to care for the family for 3 weeks. Mollie's dad showed up for a few days, stayed in a nearby hotel and left with Kate.

During that time, Mollie had been In touch with Robin and June. When Robin talked money, it was a raise but not of the magnitude of June's client. Mollie took the job with The App Store. She wrote a very nice resignation letter, thanked everyone at IBM and asked to keep her stock. Other than advice from IBM's stock plan administrator, we heard nothing. Mollie put all of this paper in a file marked IBM which included the memo about her earlier conversation with Robin.

A number of Mollie's co-workers at IBM left to join Mollie at The App Store. Mollie was quickly appointed a manager.

50

TIME TO REFLECT

At this point in my life, my commitments began to weigh heavily on me. I knew, subconsciously at least, that I was drinking too much, not getting enough exercise and beginning to put on a bit of weight. At the start of 1986, I took up running at lunchtime, so I replaced cocktails and food with wholesome exercise (except most of the running was on sidewalks and streets- bad cumulative outcome pending!). That helped, but my mental outlook worsened.

Dr. Arnaud wanted me to stop trying to please so many different people. When I told her about Gerry, after the 3d time, she was simply outraged! Somehow because Carolyn came before my real romance with Mollie and other factors, those occasional trysts did not seem to bother the good doctor. (In fact, in the great decline in physical love life with Mollie, Dr. Arnaud asked me several times about Carolyn's whereabouts creating the impression for me that my psychiatrist thought my having a mistress of sorts was a good idea.) She virtually insisted that I break off the relationship with Gerry.

Carolyn was busy all over the place earning money and fame. I could hardly pass a magazine stand without seeing her All-American face on a cover. And she had Patrick and Violet back in Connecticut. So, if I saw her in the flesh twice/year, that was a lot.

Because of all my law practice commitments, I was able to get the Pacific Area Reserve Chief to agree that I could do 16 weekends/year instead of 12 weekends and 2 weeks of active duty. I had hit the point where I was no longer being paid. That helped, but I needed all of this drill time to retire with full medical benefits and some retirement pay at age 60. To fill my time that senior captain asked that I spend those weekends getting all of the Western USCG Reservists, especially those in California, to have all of their paperwork in order in the event they were called to active duty. This meant that about half of those weekends would be out of the Bay Area, even Northern CA.

The Asbestos law work was exciting and I was exploring options with the client and Desert Mutual to reduce the current Bodily Injury caseload and to forestall a growth of new filings for the future. Then came the cases that were to change my life forever. CAL Board was served with a class action to remove all of its asbestos products from all of the primary and secondary schools in America. Two weeks later the Los Angeles Unified School District (LAUSD), the biggest in the U.S., filed a similar suit. The former was venued in federal court in Philadelphia and the latter in California state court in Los Angeles. Manny and Gerry wanted me to direct all of this litigation as well. This meant more time with Gerry and on the road.

All of this also meant more stress. Little did I know that it was all just beginning to build!!

51

DR. ARNAUD: A REFLECTION

*F*or all the years that we consulted, I always addressed you as Dr. Arnaud. Our first meetings which ran together long ago helped to shape the rest of my life. As of now, my walk-away included: *think of others' feelings, but always consider how yours are shaped by what you will do; never act out of malice alone; really caring, really matters, so be careful for whom or what you really care; thinking first is the key to all decision-making; and, try to have an ethical basis to which you can relate any " hard "decision before you make it.*

Not one of those phrases ever left your lips, or, to the best of my memory, were uttered by me. Yet, I shall always think of them, and their corollaries, as evolving from my early years with you. That said: they have served me well in my personal life, and especially in the practice of law - the ethical practice of law!

SAUSALITO

A SPECIAL EPILOG

My activities with Gerry Dwyer at the Palace Hotel began to cause me worriment after a few of these assignations. Although she was enthusiastic, intelligent, attractive and artful, I did not really feel any emotional attachment for her as I did with Carolyn, Sandra, and eventually, then completely, with Mollie. Dr. Arnaud was beside herself when I explained what I had been up to. My assertion that Gerry had seduced me was met with, "Tell me again how you just happened to go up to her room after drinks, dinner, and MORE drinks?" Certainly no empathy from my psychiatrist! Just guilt.

Almost two weeks after that session, there was another day of deposition that Gerry was going to attend. We met that morning when I picked her up at the New Montgomery Street Palace entrance and we headed to Oakland. She provided gossip from Desert Mutual on the way to the parking structure in Downtown Oakland and in 2 short blocks, we were at the court reporter office where they had laid out a small repast for the 20+ lawyers and the witness. Gerry was the only client, but Mr. Granger was the key witness for her company. Wallboard's lawyer was taking the continued deposition of its former Risk Manager that day. Instead of Talbot Allen resuming where he left of the week before, who should show up but his daughter, Sandra.

We were cool but cordial during introductions. The Bay Area lawyers mostly knew of our past relationship, but not the L.A. lawyers. I introduced Gerry to Sandra, clients are allowed to attend absent a court order barring them. Gerry's, "Nice to meet you. Ronan's told me nice things about you...," seemed to fall on Sandra's deaf ears.

The day proved unremarkable as despite innumerable tactics, Sandra could not shake Millard Granger's position that Wallboard had agreed there would be no coverage for asbestos with Desert Mutual, that "asbestosis" was used as a term by all concerned to cover all asbestos related diseases, and that he, on behalf of the party desperate for primary coverage, would draft the exclusion to protect Desert Mutual. When we adjourned at day's end, Sandra allowed that Wallboard would have more questions next week. Gerry turned and smiled at me.

When we got my car onto the Nimitz Freeway headed toward the Bay Bridge, Gerry said, "The gossip this morning was just a beginning. There are going to be even more changes in Desert Mutual Home Claims. I know, and now you do as well. You see, I am leaving. The Hartford wants me to go to Connecticut and get a firm grip on their asbestos claims which appear to be mounting at an out of control rate. For the money they offered, not to mention the title and prestige, I could hardly refuse. I will make my announcement tomorrow afternoon when I get back to the office. So, tonight, how about if we just do drinks? I need to be well rested for tomorrow."

I was more than a bit stunned by the news, but quickly acquiesced as this path seemed almost miraculous for bringing about a friendly end to this unwanted relationship. At the Pied Piper Bar, after her second double Martini, Gerry waffled and hinted that once more would be great. I tried being her conscience and she somewhat surprisingly agreed to forego what might seemed "a bit forced under the circumstances." Her parting words stay with me, "You taught me a lot about claims, lawsuits and tactics, but even more about good sex. Thank you for everything!" and she put her hand out for me to shake it.

I did.

FINAL EPILOGUE

I break here as my world, complex as it might appear to this point, will only become far more complicated in its personal and professional relationships which I will hope to relate in a future work, having spent 5 years getting this far.

Ronan O'Neill January 2017

ABOOKS

ALIVE Book Publishing and ALIVE Publishing Group
are imprints of Advanced Publishing LLC,
3200 A Danville Blvd., Suite 204, Alamo, California 94507

Telephone: 925.837.7303
alivebookpublishing.com